The Second Mrs. Darcy

Renata McMann &
Summer Hanford

Other Pride and Prejudice variations by Renata McMann

Heiress to Longbourn
Pemberley Weddings
The Inconsistency of Caroline Bingley
Three Daughters Married
Anne de Bourgh Manages
The above works are collected in the book
Five Pride and Prejudice Variations

Also by Renata McMann
Journey Towards a Preordained Time

Short Stories by Summer Hanford
The Forging of Cadwel
Hawk Trials for Mirimel
The Fall of Larkesong

Novels by Summer Hanford
Gift of the Aluien
Hawks of Sorga
Throne of Wheylia

Cover by Summer Hanford

Contents

ISBN-13: 978-1500763503
ISBN-10: 1500763500

Chapter 1

Darcy handed Elizabeth the letter. He tried to catch her eyes, to express with a look what he couldn't speak aloud, but she avoided his gaze. Marshaling himself, he gave her a brief bow and left.

At least she took the letter. He suspected curiosity would make her read it, especially as his method of delivery safeguarded her reputation. He hoped, with a quiet desperation, that she wouldn't simply toss it on the fire. Even though he'd ruined his chanced with her already, he needed her to know the truth, so that she wouldn't think on him too harshly.

It had taken him hours to write the letter, but he said everything he needed to say. He wrote about Wickham's infamous behavior, even though it meant exposing his sister Georgiana's near elopement. He explained that he'd persuaded Bingley not to marry Elizabeth's sister, Jane Bennet, largely because he believed she didn't love Bingley, but would accept an offer of marriage because of his wealth. He poured his heart into the letter and now he felt he had no heart left. He never loved a woman before he met Elizabeth Bennet, and never would again.

He walked back to Rosings, hardly noticing his surroundings. What were the beauties of nature to a man who would never see love in Elizabeth's eyes? Darcy's lips curled, caught between self-mocking and pain at his own lovelorn thoughts. He was become the very type of man he once decried.

"Cousin," said a quiet voice.

"Anne," he said, turning to find his cousin, Anne de Bourgh, seated on a shade-dappled bench beneath an ancient oak, a blanket over her lap. Surprised to find her alone, Darcy looked around until he spotted her companion, Mrs. Jenkinson. She occupied another bench, a fair distance away across the well-groomed lawn, shrewd eyes fixed on them over her sewing.

Anne's gaze followed his and she said, "I was indulging in the illusion of privacy, but I don't mind your company. Will you join me?"

Darcy didn't feel like company, but nothing else would suit his mood, either. There was no point in being churlish to Anne, he thought, seating himself next to her, thinking about how yesterday he himself had indulged. His illusions were of spending time with Elizabeth at his side, basking in her ardor and gratitude. He'd expected to be planning a wedding, but instead he saw the rest of his days lined up before him, empty.

He spent weeks persuading himself a marriage for love was worth all the disadvantages it brought. In his arrogance, and he could now see it as such after her humbling treatment, he hadn't realizing that he was not the one who needed persuading. If he'd spent a tenth of the time in courting Elizabeth that he had in arguing with himself he might...

Darcy sighed. No, he would never have changed her mind, but at least he would have known she didn't want him. At least he could have spared his pride. What a fool he'd been to assume she was his for the asking.

"What troubles you?" Anne asked.

Darcy didn't answer immediately. He didn't want to add to Anne's burdens by discussing his own. Her continued ill health was something she didn't complain of, but must be hard to bear. His mind floundered, unable to think of any words that didn't involve Elizabeth. He turned to her, taking in the concern in her eyes, and realized that he'd waited too long to speak. Now she would never believe him if he told her he was fine.

"Don't tell me it's nothing, because I know it's something. You can tell me. Mrs. Jenkinson isn't within hearing and there are no servants about. I promise not to repeat what you say to me."

Darcy knew that was true, since Anne kept to herself, but he still couldn't form an answer. As much as he wished to unburden himself, it bore the risk of Anne's censure. She might side with Elizabeth. He was uncertain if his bruised ego could endure further chastening.

Anne's took in his reluctance to speak. "Sometimes, I sit here and sing to myself," she said, not pressing him. It wasn't her way to press, for which Darcy was grateful. "I sing very badly. I wish I sang like Miss Bennet."

Darcy jerked at her name. Memories of her at the piano

4

warred with ruined dreams of her voice accompanying Georgiana's playing, filling Pemberley with sound and joy.

"Don't you like Miss Bennet's singing?" Anne asked. "I love it."

"So do I," Darcy said, unwilling to lie.

"Why did you react so strongly?" Her eyes searched his face, holding his gaze.

"I didn't." Darcy saw Anne didn't believe him. He could read the hurt on her face as he lied. He didn't want to add treating his cousin poorly to his list of sins. Besides, who could he tell, if not Anne? "That is, I love more than her singing," he said, the admission nearly catching in his throat.

"But you won't marry her because she is so beneath you?" Anne asked, her eyes still holding his gaze.

Darcy realized his earlier supposition was correct. His cousin would side with Elizabeth, and be right to. "I won't marry her because she won't marry me," he said. He managed the pronouncement in an even tone, his steadiness belying the pain it caused him to utter the words.

"You asked her?" she said in a tone of mild surprise.

"Last night," he said, reflecting that his cousin's surprise underscored how badly he'd conducted his courtship, if a courtship he could name it. "She refused me in terms... Well, let's say that I'm the last man in the world she would marry."

"I'm sorry she was so harsh with you," Anne said. "I wouldn't think she would be so impolite. She parried my mother's ill manners without bowing to her, in spite of Mama's provocation."

"I provoked her more," Darcy said. As bitter as the memory of his behavior was, he couldn't help but reflect on the irony, that he should defend a decision which wounded him so deeply. "I insulted her when I proposed. I was so sure she would accept that I thought it was more important to explain why I delayed so long in proposing than it was to woo her. She had every right to insult me."

"Perhaps if you give her time and try again," Anne said, the sympathy in her voice wounding him. "Now that you know she needs to be wooed, woo her. If you love her, it will be worth it."

"She will never love me," Darcy said. "I thought her witticisms were directed at me because she was flirting with me. I was wrong. She was trying to throw barbs at me because she didn't like me, not realizing how I misinterpreted them. She disliked me from the beginning and last night I fulfilled all of her negative expectations. She is out of my life, and she is probably grateful for that. I care too much to inflict my presence on her. Since she can't be my wife, I want her to be happy, and the only way I can do that is by staying away."

He clamped his mouth shut, realizing he'd grown impassioned in his speech. He hadn't meant to reveal his pain so fully, even to Anne. Would this raw feeling, this anger and grief, always live inside him now, lurking below the surface of civility, waiting to burst forth?

To his relief, Anne didn't respond, giving him time to reassert control as they sat in silence. He tried to turn his mind to other things - his business ventures, Georgiana, Pemberley - but his mind kept turning back to Elizabeth. Pemberley should have an heir and his former visions of Elizabeth holding their child mocked him. She would marry, probably within a year or two. She would find some local squire, or worse, a clerk or tradesman where poverty and toil would wear her down. He hoped whoever it was would appreciate her wit, beauty and kindness. He once thought she was unworthy of him, but by turning him down, she proved herself above all of the self-interested women who fawned on him.

He stared morosely at the ground, mind filled with a vision of how lovely Elizabeth looked, even as she denied him. He would never love again.

"If you had married her this summer, you might have had a son who would reach his majority before you were fifty," Anne mused, braking into his gloomy silence.

"I hadn't thought of it in those terms," Darcy said, surprised by his cousin's line of reason.

"I have. My father died at fifty. So did yours."

"My father didn't live long enough to help Georgiana find a husband," Darcy said, trying to orient his mind to her turn in conversation.

Anne gave a bitter laugh. "My father wanted me to have a season in London. He even told me that it didn't matter if I didn't find anyone, because I could have as many seasons as I wanted. He said he didn't really want to give me to some man who wouldn't appreciate me."

"You were sixteen when he died?" Darcy asked, trying to remember. He was sorry his father died before Georgiana was settled and realized he wanted to live to see his children grow up and marry. Yet, without Elizabeth…

"Yes," Anne said, cutting into his desolate thoughts. "We spent a year in mourning, and then I got sick and couldn't come out. It was only then that Mama decided I was engaged to you."

6

"We weren't…"

"No. We never were. I want to marry, but Mama doesn't allow anyone here who will court me."

"I would think you would fear childbirth," Darcy said. He regretted saying it, thinking it too intimate, even for cousins. Why had he never before realized, until Elizabeth pointed it out, that he was such an unmitigated lout?

"No. I want children or at least a child," Anne said, apparently unruffled by his poor manners. "I know I'm sickly, but if I can survive childbirth, a wet nurse can take care of my child. Even if I don't survive, I'll leave something behind. I grow weaker every year. I'm afraid, very afraid, that when I die there will be nothing left of me. The world will never know I even lived. I don't want that. And there's Rosings. Who would inherit it? I would love it to be my child, even if I'm not there to see it."

"Are you sure?" Darcy asked.

"Yes. Very. I want a child, even if it kills me." She turned earnest eyes on him. "I want to live, not stay wrapped in a cocoon. What sort of life is this? Better to live only a year more, were it a good one, than go on watching my days slip away along with any chance I have of ever being strong enough to enjoy them."

Darcy took in the quiet intensity of her tone. He realized he loved his sweet frail cousin. Not passionately, and not enough, but he'd lost that kind of love the moment Elizabeth refused him. There was real fear in Anne's eyes and, he saw, real hope. This was not idle conversation. Her words were not spoken by chance.

Part of his mind said he was crazy to do this, but he knew he couldn't marry for love. He might as well marry for caring, for family and for fortune. He slipped to one knee, the gravel around the bench crunching under his weight, and proposed marriage to Anne. He ended it by saying, "I can't promise you my heart, but I will treat you with respect."

Anne agreed with Darcy's request that they keep their engagement secret until Elizabeth Bennet left Kent. Darcy told her, his face showing his concern at her reaction, that he didn't want to belittle Elizabeth by letting her know he proposed to another woman so soon after his declaration of love for her. Anne nodded, accepting that what he said was true. She didn't have his heart, but she had his obligation, and that was all she required.

They did nearly quarrel, however, when Anne requested permission to inform her mother of Darcy's proposal to Elizabeth. Darcy didn't see the need. Anne explained, nearly resorting to tears, how difficult it would be to obtain the concessions he wished for from her mother without sharing the knowledge. Once she made him fully aware of how much her mother would press for a large wedding and all of the appropriate fanfare, should she think Darcy truly in love with Anne, she had no trouble obtaining his permission to approach the matter as she thought best.

Once that was agreed, he left for London to arrange for a special license and for settlements to be drawn up. After he left, Anne sought out her mother, who was in her sitting room. She paused before knocking and entering, schooling from her face her satisfaction at how well she managed Darcy. She still had to face her mother.

"What brings you here?" Lady Catherine said, looking up from the book she held.

"I wanted to talk to you in private, about Darcy," Anne said. She held in her excitement. It was a rare occurrence, this opportunity to shock her mother.

"I'm sure he will agree to marry next year. There is no reason to give up. You were formed for each other." Her mother sounded belligerent, as if she could command her wishes into fact.

"He's already agreed," Anne said, savoring the astonishment that suffused Lady Catherine's face. "He's arranging for a special license and for settlements to be drawn up. We will get married privately next week."

"What! You didn't consult me," her mother said. Her tone took on that aggrieved note that cut across Anne's nerves like a poorly played violin.

"Mama, I am an adult," Anne said. She held her mother's gaze, not looking down as she normally would. This was too important for her usual meekness. "My dowry will be divided into three equal parts. I will have one third, one third will be set aside for any children, and he will get the final third. This isn't at Darcy's urging, but I would like you to sign something saying that if I die before you do, and I have a child, that the child will inherit Rosings."

Lady Catherine was nonplused by this, looking at a loss for words. After a few moments, she said, "Rosings will already go to your children by your father's will. I deem your stipulations entirely reasonable. But why the secrecy, why the speed?"

"I'm not well enough to want a big wedding," Anne said, relieved and a bit surprised that her mother wasn't arguing with her. It wasn't that her requests were in any way unreasonable. She was simply accustomed to her mother being contrary and giving orders for the sake of ordering. She pressed for more while the shock of the happy news was still curbing her mother's tongue. "I want to go to my new home quietly and quickly and live there. Darcy thinks I should spend some time in London first and buy my trousseau."

"I'll pay for your trousseau," Lady Catherine said. "I'll send an announcement to the newspaper too, or is Darcy attending to it?"

"No. I don't want an announcement, at least not for a while." Seeing her mother's frown, Anne hastened to add, "Darcy will be embarrassed if Miss Bennet reads about his marriage so soon."

"What has Miss Bennet to do with this?" her mother asked, her tone sharp. "I know she was attempting to use her arts and allurements to entrap my nephew, but we should not consider her at all."

"Mama, I owe this all to her. Darcy would never have proposed to me if he hadn't been refused by her."

"What!" Her mother was clearly horrified by the notion. Pink spots formed on her cheeks, bright enough to show through her layers of powder.

"He proposed to her and she refused. What's more, she refused in terms that made it clear he could never win her." She could no longer contain her smugness. "I'm so happy, Mama. I've waited years for this and that silly girl doesn't know what kind of husband she gave up. I'm grateful to her. I would have relinquished my dowry to achieve this and it was given to me for free."

"You mean to say that Darcy proposed and she refused?" her mother asked, apparently too horrified by the idea to set it aside. "I didn't think she had enough sense of class to realize how far beneath him she was."

"That is the jest," Anne said, gleeful. "Neither she nor Darcy considers her beneath him. She refused because she didn't like him enough to marry him. If she visits here again, you must be particularly nice to her. Even if she never thought of me, she did me a great kindness. Now, set down your reading and come congratulate me."

Darcy knew it was a mistake within an hour of his proposal. He could see his behavior for the grief-spurred reaction it was. A sinking feeling was added to his sorrow over losing Elizabeth, for he'd neatly trapped himself. That a single irrational moment should lead to such an extraordinary alteration in his life seemed hardly fair for one who prided himself on a demeanor of reason and contemplation.

Yet, he was honor bound to stand by his word, especially

once he gave Anne permission to tell Lady Catherine. It wouldn't be too bad. Anne would be an undemanding wife. She was always quiet, nearly invisible. Such a contrast, he thought, to Elizabeth. Angrily, Darcy pushed such comparisons from his mind.

With his cousin Fitzwilliam safely attending to his military duties, there was no one to check Darcy's headlong lunge into married life, nor shame him by observing it. Within a week of his proposal, Darcy welcomed Anne and Lady Catherine to Darcy House. After two days of dealing with legal documents, Anne Catherine de Bourgh and Fitzwilliam George Darcy were married in a private ceremony. Darcy tried to smile at her as they signed the papers, but his face felt nearly as numb as his heart.

As if to prove the reassurances he gave himself, Anne asked for only one thing. She wanted to bring several servants and a few pieces of furniture from Rosings, a reasonable request. His whole marriage, possibly the rest of his life, would be this way, he realized. Quiet, reasonable and numb. That was what life without Elizabeth was.

The wedding night brought new torments to Darcy. In his mind, though he desperately tried not to, he couldn't help but picture Elizabeth. Worse still, Anne did nothing to distract from visions of her. Anne tolerated him, but obviously took no pleasure in consummating their union. She seemed uninterested in enjoying their time together. She didn't reject him, nor hint at a rejection, but she showed no signs of pleasure.

Darcy knew he was hardly the first man to find his wife was passionless, but he had no intention of enjoying his ample opportunities to sate such appetites elsewhere. That wasn't the Darcy way. Still, he would have been hard pressed to return to her bedside anytime soon, were the main purpose of his marriage was not to produce an heir. Yet another way, his mind whispered, that life would surely have been better with Elizabeth. If only … Darcy clenched his jaw, refusing to finish the thought. He would not dwell in departed dreams. That, too, was not the Darcy way.

Chapter 2

Elizabeth couldn't believe she'd agreed to visit Pemberley. Mr. and Mrs. Gardiner wanted to see it, and Elizabeth couldn't object without explaining, though she felt surely her mortification must shine from her face. Her salvation was the serving girl at the inn. She was sure that Darcy wasn't in residence, allowing Elizabeth to agree without having to decide if declining was worth telling her aunt and uncle why she didn't want to go.

They started the tour of the house with a very pleasant housekeeper, Mrs. Reynolds, who'd barely shown them one room when she received a message brought by a footman. Whatever it was, she apologized and the rest of the tour was taken over by the largely silent footman, who said nothing, simply escorting them around.

Not that many words were needed, for Pemberley spoke for itself. The rooms combined beauty, elegance and comfort. Elizabeth was impressed in spite of all the other magnificent houses she'd seen over the last weeks. Pemberley exceeded her expectations.

After they finished seeing those rooms permissible to the public, their conscripted tour guide turned them over to a groundskeeper. He did a better job as a guide, but only spoke of the grounds, not of the inhabitants of the house. Of course, Elizabeth sternly reminded herself, she did not care about the inhabitants of Pemberley.

She tried not to count how many times during the tour she was forced to reiterate that thought, though it became less and less necessary as the beauty of the grounds enfolded her. She felt she could hardly recall her own name, transported by natural wonders as she was, let alone her inner turmoil. Still, an image of Darcy's face as she last saw it, when he handed her the note, refused to dissipate, tormenting her as she traversed his home.

She felt guilty for misjudging him and for refusing him so harshly. She still believed he was a rude man who thought himself above his company, but he wasn't a bad man. She really didn't want him to renew his addresses. Life with him would be difficult and he probably wouldn't allow her to see her family. The honor of being the Mistress of Pemberley was not worth being the wife of Mr. Darcy.

When they finished, with Elizabeth and her relatives quite thoroughly impressed by Pemberley, they proceeded to their carriage. Before they reached it, however, another carriage swept up the tree-lined drive. Elizabeth's breath caught in her throat when Mr. Darcy alighted, looking in every way as dashing as she recalled. It was all she could do to keep putting one foot before the other as she trailed her aunt and uncle. What would Mr. Darcy think, finding her in his home? Would he think she was pursuing him?

After reading his letter, handed to her over three months ago, it didn't take her long to acquit him of guilt in his dealings with Wickham, and she accepted that he behaved reasonably in his separating Bingley from her sister. Where once her uncensored abrading of him had filled her with something approaching pride, she now felt renewed shame over her behavior. She ducked her head, focusing her gaze on the stones of the drive. Maybe he wouldn't see her.

In the edge of her vision, she could see he was helping someone from the carriage and she found herself looking up, curious as to whom. Elizabeth realized it must be Georgiana Darcy, from her resemblance to her brother. In spite of her foreknowledge, she was surprised at how very young and innocent the girl looked, bolstering her dislike of Wickham.

As neither brother nor sister seemed aware anyone approached, Elizabeth kept her gaze raised, intrigued when the normally unsociable Mr. Darcy reached back inside the coach, another delicate gloved hand clasping his. To Elizabeth's surprise, the next occupant Darcy helped out was Anne de Bourgh. Where neither Darcy nor his sister looked at her, Miss de Bourgh's gaze fell on her immediately and she said, "Good morning, Miss Bennet."

Having no choice, Elizabeth altered her course toward them, fixedly refusing to let herself take in Mr. Darcy's face. Approaching Anne, she curtsied. "Good morning, Miss de Bourgh. We didn't mean to intrude. We were just leaving," she said, hoping her tone was unrevealing. She was fully unprepared for the feelings that churned in her at being so near Mr. Darcy. They were of such a nearly violent cast, she was uncertain, even, of their nature.

"Oh, but you can't leave," Anne de Bourgh said, more effusive than Elizabeth remembered. "Please, come inside and take some refreshment. I was so delighted to know you at Rosings. Please introduce me to your friends, as well. And I am not Miss de Bourgh anymore, I'm Mrs. Darcy."

Elizabeth was so startled by this news that she couldn't protest. Mechanically, she performed the introductions. Anne Darcy said more in a few seconds of their meeting than she'd said in six weeks at Rosings, and of such import! Dazed by the news, Elizabeth couldn't help being overcome by Mrs. Darcy's insistence that they stay.

A few minutes later, they found themselves in a pleasant room with a view of the woods. It hadn't been part of the tour, and Elizabeth could see why. If she had such a perfect room as her own, she wouldn't want to share it with strangers either. She let her eyes stay on to the view, taking in the deep cool shade offered by the sweeping boughs, wishing she could lose her person there as well. She realized her aunt and uncle were making polite conversation, but couldn't bring herself to join in.

"Would you care to play, Miss Bennet?" Georgiana's tentative voice broke into the numbing haze that seemed to have enveloped Elizabeth. The girl cast a look at her brother, as if seeking support. "Only, my brother and Mrs. Darcy both speak so highly of your playing. I should love to hear it."

"Yes, of course," Elizabeth said, fighting to urge to look to Darcy herself, for confirmation of the compliment. A new emotion surged in her, one she could readily identify. How dare he be married so soon after declaring his love for her? Did Anne Darcy know he'd proposed to her? Elizabeth stood, her posture ridged, and gestured for Georgiana to precede her.

Elizabeth was pleased the pianoforte was in an adjoining room, not so close to Darcy. Georgiana sorted through several sheets, reading the titles, until she found music Elizabeth was familiar with. Elizabeth settled onto the bench, forcing herself to focus on the notes. She didn't want to think about the unexpected marriage of Mr. Darcy to Anne de Bourgh, so she lost herself in the music.

When she finished, she decided to play the piece again, apologizing to Georgiana for being out of practice. Soon enough, her second rendition was complete. It seemed even playing the piece twice couldn't keep her from the Darcy's. Georgiana's complements filling her ears, she left the instrument and returned to the others, politely thanking Miss Darcy.

When she reentered the sitting room, her uncle was asking Mr. Darcy about fishing, a topic that occupied the two men for several minutes. Mr. Darcy invited him, with the greatest civility, to fish in his stream as often as he chose while he continued in the neighborhood, offering at the same time to supply him with fishing tackle, and pointing out those parts of the stream where there was usually the most sport.

While the men talked, the four women remained silent. Elizabeth earnestly tried to think of something to say, but her mind was full of question too forward to ask. She gazed down at her hands, wondering why her aunt had selected this moment to be so quiet. Their lack of conversation was beginning to border on the admonishable.

"Miss Bennet," Georgiana Darcy said, surprising Elizabeth by being the one to break the silence. "I've only just recollected that, while in London, my music teacher had me work on a duet. She said I should play my part every day. Would you like to help me practice?"

Elizabeth smiled, more than happy for an excuse to return to the piano. She nodded, rising, but what she truly wished to do was to thank Georgiana. It seemed wrong that the youngest among them must be the one to end such an awkward interval, but Elizabeth would take relief where it was offered.

As they played, the two women didn't say much, and nothing that didn't relate to the music, but Elizabeth enjoyed herself and found it preferable to being so near to Mr. and Mrs. Darcy. She wondered at the level of civility she was receiving from the man whose proposal she so harshly, and unjustly, rejected. Equally surprising was the civility of his second choice, but then, surely Anne Darcy could not know.

Darcy determined to talk politely to Elizabeth's relatives, regardless of how crude they were. He focused himself on that resolve, keeping both mind and eyes from contemplation of Elizabeth, who seemed only to have grown lovelier since last they met. A part of him wished, as well, to show her that he had taken her words to heart, but his resolution turned out to be easy to keep. Elizabeth's aunt and uncle were intelligent, well-informed, and pleasant. Anne, for her part, said nothing, but that was expected.

Feeling himself straying toward a comparison between Anne and Elizabeth, he launched into a discourse on the fine fishing his estate offered. As if to further tempt him, sounds of music, and even merriment, drifted from the other room as Georgiana and Elizabeth worked on the duet. Darcy fancied he could separate which notes were played by his sister, and which were struck by Miss Bennet.

When a particularly lovely strand of Elizabeth's laughter crossed the space between them, seeming almost to brighten the very room, Darcy glanced at Anne in concern. He couldn't fathom why she had invited Elizabeth and her relatives in. Surely, it must be awkward for Anne, having Elizabeth in their home. In fact, Elizabeth was there when they arrived, meaning she had now spent more time in Pemberley than Anne had, since their marriage.

By all regards, Anne appeared to be paying attention to the conversation at hand, showing no signs of being distracted by happenings in the adjourning room. When Mrs. Gardiner asked Anne a question, she answered promptly and appropriately. Could Anne truly be complacent with Elizabeth's presence in their home? Darcy knew Anne was fond of Miss Bennet, but he hadn't realized how far her regard extended.

Turning his own attention more firmly to the conversation, he decided he should follow her example. It was easier to do than he anticipated, since the Gardiners were enjoyable conversationalists. So much so, he could scarcely credit that they were of the same family as Elizabeth's mother. After an acceptable half an hour, Mrs. Gardiner arose, saying they must be going, since their dinner was bespoken at the inn.

"Please stay for dinner at Pemberley," Anne said, eliciting a level of surprise in Darcy that he hoped did not show on his face. "Miss Darcy is usually shy with strangers and she's getting along so well with Miss Bennet. We can send a message to the inn."

Both young women laughed at something in the other room. Mrs. Gardiner glanced at her husband, who nodded his acceptance. Darcy knew he couldn't protest without being terribly rude and undercutting Anne's new role as mistress of the house. Hearing Elizabeth and Georgiana playing in the adjoining room, he wasn't sure he wanted to protest. It was good to have her there, in his home, acquainting herself with his sister, and Anne was right. Georgiana seemed to have taken a particular liking to Elizabeth, as Darcy always knew she would. If Anne found the situation acceptable, he decided, he did as well.

Dinner proved more trying than Darcy anticipated. It began somewhat informally, with Anne ignoring precedence by placing Elizabeth and Georgiana on either side of her. This not only left Darcy with the Gardiners, but put Elizabeth at the other end of the table, where it was difficult to keep his eyes from straying to her. Each time he realized he was looking at Elizabeth, he quickly moved his gaze to Anne. He hoped he was taken for a love-struck new husband.

He met Anne's gaze across the length of the table, smiling at her. He owed it to his wife and his guests to be a good host. This was

Anne's first night as mistress of Pemberley, their first three months of marriage having been spent in London. Whatever his manners were elsewhere, Darcy knew at Pemberley he must attend to his guests, though the Gardiners made that attention an enjoyable duty. The three women at the opposite end of the table also seemed to get along well, with Elizabeth and Georgiana talking about music. Anne had little to say but appeared pleased.

To have guests on the first day was unusual. After the Gardiners accepted her invitation, Anne had called for Mrs. Reynolds and told her there were three more for dinner. By her unruffled demeanor, Darcy concluded that Anne assumed Mrs. Reynolds would cope. Anne was right in this, but her calm confidence in the competency of the staff surprised Darcy. It was, he reflected, in the nature of a compliment to him, which pleased him.

After dinner, Mrs. Reynolds caught his eye. Mr. Darcy excused himself, indicating that Mr. Gardiner should join the ladies. As Mr. Gardiner followed a servant to a sitting room, Mrs. Reynolds told Mr. Darcy that the footman who notified the inn that the Gardiners were at Pemberley, had returned with two letters for Miss Bennet. She hadn't wished to interrupt dinner with them. Darcy agreed to that, but suggested she take them to Elizabeth now, knowing how she enjoyed hearing from her family.

Elizabeth took the first letter and started reading it, excusing herself from the conversation around her and turning slightly away from Georgiana, who sat beside her on a couch. At first there was a slight smile on her face, which pleased Darcy, but then she gasped, stilling the talk in the room. After quickly perusing the rest of the document, she handed the first letter to her aunt, hurriedly tearing open the second. The remaining people watched the two women read the letters. Mrs. Gardiner passed the letter to her husband, saying "Start here," and pointing halfway down the page.

"Poor Lydia!" Elizabeth exclaimed, clutching the second letter to her chest. There were tears in her eyes. "Uncle, I simply must return home."

"What is the matter," Darcy asked, half rising from his chair.

"Family business," Mr. Gardiner said. "I'm sorry, but we have to leave immediately."

"What can I do to help?" Darcy asked, taking in how stricken Elizabeth looked.

"Just order our carriage." Mr. Gardiner, so far an exceedingly self-assured man, sounded nearly as rattled as Elizabeth looked.

"Of course, but by the time you pick up your belongings you

16

won't make much progress. We could send for them and you could stay here for the night. We are south of Lambton," Anne said, ringing for a servant.

"We could hardly impose," Mr. Gardiner said, shaking his head.

"It's no imposition," Anne said. "Pemberley has plenty of room."

"Is there any other way we could be of service?" Darcy asked. "Is Lydia ill? I could send my London doctor."

"It isn't anything like that," said Mr. Gardiner, gruffly, dropping his gaze.

Darcy could see that Elizabeth and the Gardiners didn't wish to share the details of their news. There was a brief awkward silence, broken when a servant came into the room. Darcy looked from Mr. Gardiner to Mrs. Gardiner, wondering if they would consent to Anne's offer of accommodations.

After a glance at her husband, Mrs. Gardiner said, "We accept with gratitude."

Darcy ordered the servant to pick up the belongings of the Gardiners, but Mrs. Gardiner suggested it would be easier if she could go and pack. Elizabeth offered to go along and help. The round trip would bring them back at dusk, meaning that time would be saved, since it was unlikely they could make much progress that evening. Darcy, Mr. Gardiner, and Georgiana went to see the carriage off. Anne, as was her custom, didn't venture out of doors unnecessarily.

Chapter 3

Elizabeth was grateful that practical matters kept her busy until the carriage left Lambton to return to Pemberley, since it didn't give her time to dwell on her thoughts. Mrs. Gardiner stayed long enough to write notes to her friends in Lambton, which meant it was after sunset when they pulled up to Pemberley.

Elizabeth spent the journey wondering about what Lydia's elopement with Wickham would mean to her and her family. She knew from Darcy's letter that Wickham was untrustworthy. It was unlikely he would marry a woman with no fortune, and marriage was the only respectable end to this. If Lydia and Wickham didn't marry, she and her sisters would be tainted by the scandal.

She was grateful Darcy treated her so well. The acrimony of her refusal to his marriage proposal gave him every reason to confine his behavior to a polite greeting, if that. Yet, she realized, not wanting to read too much into his behavior, it wasn't Darcy who invited her and her family to Pemberley, but his wife. Darcy did treat her aunt and uncle well, better than she expected him to treat anyone in trade. He was friendly and open with them.

She didn't flatter herself that her reproofs caused him to change his behavior. Perhaps it was because he was in his home, but she rather thought it was marriage that changed him. Married life clearly suited Mr. Darcy.

What was it about the men whose proposals she rejected? Was she some sort of gateway to finding the correct woman? Mr. Collins proposed to Charlotte a scant three days after he proposed to her. How long did Darcy wait? Was it three days or was it longer?

Darcy waved goodbye to Elizabeth and the Gardiners, who left as soon as it was light. He wondered what befell Lydia, not that he cared about her, but Elizabeth was in distress. He wanted to help her, but he had no right. He gave up any hope of helping her when he married Anne. Watching their carriage dwindle down the drive, he was struck by how right it had seemed to have Elizabeth in

Pemberley, and how despairingly empty his home already felt without her.

Manfully, he strived to press such thoughts from his head. It wasn't Anne's fault that he didn't love her. It also wasn't her fault that her health was poor. He went into the marriage knowing the truth of both those things. Anne lived up to her part of the bargain. She was his wife, and they sometimes shared a bed. She listened to what he said and commented on it. Yet, she almost never ventured an opinion or initiated a topic of conversation, leaving their discourse discouragingly barren.

Darcy turned on his heels and strode inside, putting more force into his steps than strictly necessary. That he ached for Elizabeth, he couldn't deny. As he walked, he didn't see the familiar halls of Pemberley, his mind replaying her every expression, the sound of her laughter in his home, the effortless grace of her form. Seeing her again opened a wound that he thought was healing.

To his surprise, Anne, not customarily such an early riser, was already at the table when he reached the dining room, though Georgiana was still absent. Not meeting Anne's eyes, he seated himself across from her. He'd promised her respect when he proposed to her, and pining over another woman was not respectful. He was unsettled by his reaction to Elizabeth. It left him feeling unreasonably disloyal.

"Fitzwilliam, I would like to speak to you privately," Anne said in her quiet voice, interrupting his thoughts.

"We are private here," he said. There were no servants in the room.

"Don't be naïve. Servant listen."

He was about to deny this, but how would he know? Anne sent a maid for her shawl, which he placed about her, marshaling himself into feeling tenderness at the sight of her overly pale and frail form. He escorted her into the garden, a place he knew she had little interest in. She clung to his arm as they walked. Glancing down, he couldn't help but notice the similarities between Anne's hand and an illustration of the bones of the human hand he saw once at university. Darcy tried to suppress a shudder, an uncharacteristic flight of fancy briefly invoking the notion that death walked at his side.

"I see I'm not the only one who finds the morning air too chill," Anne said, smiling up at him.

Darcy smiled back, disgusted with himself. Anne was a sweet person and dear to him. He had no right to harbor such unseemly comparisons in his mind. Solicitously, he escorted her to a bench in the garden, chosen because they could see if anyone was near. She settled herself and he took his place beside her. It was cool in the shade shrouding the bench, as she said, but Darcy found the morning air invigorating, not chilly.

"When you were sending off Mrs. Gardiner and Miss Bennet yesterday, I read the letters she received from her sister." Her tone perfectly matter of fact.

Darcy stiffened, all thoughts of his wife being either frail or dear expelled from his mind. He said angrily, "That was entirely improper!"

"I don't care," she said, her tone infuriatingly devoid of defensiveness or remorse. "I spent years knowing only what people told me. I finally learned to bribe the servants to bring me information. That's how I know about Wickham and your sister."

"How... How do you know?"

"You wrote a letter the night you proposed. You rang for candles and the maid who brought them took the letter to me while you were eating. You hadn't sealed it yet. Don't worry about the maid, she can't read. But I read the letter, which was why I was sitting outside waiting for you."

Darcy remembered delaying sealing the letter. He'd wanted to read it one more time to see if it said what he wanted it to say. But the content of the letter was less important than what he was finding out about the woman he married, the cousin he knew all of his life. Now, he wondered if he knew her at all. He was disgusted with her and with himself. Did he tie himself to someone with no sense of propriety? He should have known anyone Lady Catherine raised would not be bothered by the rules that applied to decent people.

Still, that wasn't the worst of it, he realized. She lay in wait for him. Her seemingly innocent questions, her apparent sympathy for his distraught state, were all a trap. He'd been lured into proposing to her. The image of her hand on his arm returned, only this time it took on the aspects of a grasping claw, vicelike.

And he had proposed, and now Anne was his wife. As unscrupulous as her methods were, he had no recourse now. He glanced sidelong at her, not trusting himself to look her full in the face without betraying disgust. She looked as demure and frail as ever. He took a deep breath, trying to master himself to civility. As her husband, he owed her that level of consideration. Yet, he couldn't sit there, seeming to condone her prying and manipulation by listening to her. He stood up and started for the house.

Anne's voice followed him. "Elizabeth's sister eloped with Wickham. It now appears as if he won't marry her."

20

Darcy stopped and turned to look at her. Her calm visage indicated she felt none of the horror of her disclosures. Perhaps she no longer had the capacity to be shocked, after years of prying into people's most private revelations. Or perhaps, in her sheltered life, she didn't realize the full import of that elopement.

"We can do something," she said, finally conveying an emotion; entreaty. "You can do something. You can use the money you received from my dowry to buy the marriage. I know you would never forgive yourself if Miss Bennet were hurt and you could have done something."

Anne was asking him to help Elizabeth? After enlightening him on the extent of her immorality, she showed unusual generosity. When he married her, he thought her of a tranquil and consistent nature. He searched her eyes, wondering, and dreading, what revelation would come next.

"I know how it looks to you," her voice quiet now, and sad, "but my mother never told me anything. I learned from the servants and only because I paid them. Mrs. Jenkinson was my mother's spy and agent. She never said anything to me in private that she couldn't say in front of my mother. I have no intention of being in the dark about what is going on around me. In London, you spoke to me of helping your sister become more sociable and enter into society, and yet you wouldn't tell me this important fact about her. I'm not going to be a good wife for you if I'm kept in the dark."

He saw her point but it was a thin excuse for her manipulation and spying. "You didn't need to know about Georgiana and Wickham in order to facilitate her coming out."

"I did," she said. "I knew little of Georgiana. She rarely ever spoke to me or in my presence. How was I to judge her character and provide suitable guidance without knowing her history?"

He frowned at her, unconvinced.

"What if, deeming her as meek and well behaved as she takes pains to appear, I was too lax in protecting her? Wickham isn't the only man who would prey on your sister. What I do is for all of our good."

Darcy continued to scowl, but her words, spinning fine filaments of reason through his head, did hold a certain amount of sense.

"I did give you your chance to be forthright with me. I asked you to tell me more about her. You talked about her music and her shyness, but never about who she is. If I spy on you, it is only because, by omission, you lie to me. That is no way to conduct this union, or to fulfill your promise of respecting me."

Darcy stared at her, aghast. He wasn't sure which was more disturbing, how much sense her argument appeared to make, on the surface, or how clear it was that she believed herself in the right. He hadn't trusted Anne enough to tell her a secret which was more Georgiana's than his.

Oddly, when he wrote the letter to Elizabeth, he trusted her more than he trusted Anne. He shook his head. He shouldn't be thinking about Elizabeth. Not right now and not that way.

He allowed anger to touch him, focusing his mind on the situation at hand. The truth was, he'd valued Georgiana's secret more than he respected Anne's ability to either keep his sister's secret or employ the information wisely. At the time, he'd felt bad about it, realizing it was unfair to Anne.

Now, he felt as if he made the right decision, even if Anne was already privy to the information. Looking down at her, huddled in her shawl on the shade-enshrouded bench, her normally self-effacing aspect transformed by conceit, Darcy realized he didn't know anything about her. She said little in private or in company. He put up with her reclusiveness in company, preferring it to a loquacious wife. He didn't mind her silences in private, finding them soothing. He realized now that what he'd thought of as companionable silences were just silences.

He'd always faced the danger that he would marry someone who pretended to be one thing and turned out to be another. He recognized that from the time he entered society. No, he realized, it was before that time. At Cambridge, he received invitations from fellow students who were more popular than he was. When he visited their homes, a sister or a cousin was almost always thrown at him. Once, one of them entered his bedchamber. He thrust her into the hallway bodily, locking the door behind her.

For years, women simpered and agreed with everything he said. He took to saying little, unless he knew the people very well. No, that wasn't a fair analysis, he thought. He was determined, after the berating Elizabeth gave him, to be honest with himself. Like his sister, he was uncomfortable in company. She hid it by visible shyness and he hid it by arrogance, but the root was the same.

Anne's eyes were still on him. Her chin tilted up, showing her arrogance and a stubbornness he never suspected. Why hadn't he tried to get to know her before he proposed? Three answers instantly came to his mind. The first was that he was in too much despair to care and the second was that he thought he did know her. The third, the one that galled him, was that her manipulation of him had been

22

artful; leading him, lamb-like, to the moment he dropped to one knee before her.

Darcy knew his wife was waiting for him to say something. He could see in her eyes that she was prepared to argue with him until he spoke words of acceptance for her machinations. Turning on his heels, he walked away.

Chapter 4

Elizabeth and the Gardiners travelled as expeditiously as possible, but as quickly as they progressed, it wasn't fast enough for Elizabeth. She stared out the window of the carriage each day, straining to glimpse the road ahead, willing the horses to go faster. She tried to comfort herself by the speed they did achieve, considering that Jane would not be wearied by long expectations, but that was scant. Sleeping one night on the road, they made it back to Hertfordshire very rapidly, reaching Longbourn by dinnertime the following day.

Elizabeth was glad that Mr. Darcy didn't know about Lydia's elopement. She sorely wished she could erase the knowledge from her own mind as well. The idea of her sister with the vile Wickham was enough to enrage and nauseate her. It would be too much for Elizabeth to bear for Darcy to know the shame of Lydia's behavior. It would be even more shameful for him to know that she eloped with Wickham.

Even though his marriage to Anne de Bourgh put him forever out of her reach, she didn't want him to think ill of her. She regretted her behavior when he proposed even more than before. Not only because seeing him again made her further question the solidity of her rejection, a painful process initiated by his letter, but because of the unfairness of her false accusations.

Added to his subsequent affable behavior at Pemberley, she was beginning to feel rather a fool, something Elizabeth was not accustomed to feeling before she set eyes on Mr. Darcy. He was all a host should be and very solicitous of his wife. Although she suspected she would still find fault with his public behavior, his behavior was exemplary in private.

More than a week after Elizabeth arrived in Longbourn, interminable days filled with her mother's and sisters' weeping, when all hope of finding the errant couple was nearly lost, a letter was sent to Longbourn signed by Lydia Wickham. She told them they were married in Scotland and Wickham would take a position as ensign in a northern regiment after resigning from the militia. Arrangements were made to cover his debts in Brighton and Meryton. The letter requested permission to visit Longbourn before they settled into their new home.

Their mother immediately recovered from the malaise she'd fallen into, refreshed with life, joy and approbation for Lydia's behavior. Mary and Kitty joined their mother's celebratory fervor. Jane was moderately pleased and optimistic about the couple's future. Elizabeth could not celebrate, since she was too baffled as to how this marriage happened. Wickham left Meryton and Brighton with many debts and suddenly he could cover them and find enough money to buy the rank of ensign? The money could not have come from the Gardiners, since they were still searching for Lydia and Wickham when the letter was received. Looking to her father, she saw a frown of puzzlement on his face, the two of them the only members of the household sensible enough for confusion.

With only questions to guide him, Elizabeth's father readily agreed to host Mr. and Mrs. Wickham at Longbourn. Elizabeth joined the other women in readying the household and in the anticipatory discomfort of waiting, though she did not join them in their frivolous happiness. She was pleased that such a potentially disastrous situation was amicably resolved, but saw no reason to forgive Lydia for her recklessness.

When Mr. and Mrs. Wickham arrived, Elizabeth's tall little sister and her ensign made a striking couple. If knowledge of their past behavior marred that image, their current behavior was enough to stoke Elizabeth's ire. Lydia was still Lydia. She demanded congratulations from everyone and planned to visit the entire village to show off her ring. There wasn't the slightest amount of shame from the couple either about the elopement or about keeping the Bennets in the dark regarding the safety of their daughter.

This vexing absence of empathy was most apparent in Lydia's lack of hesitancy in enlightening them about what happened. "It was such a lark, running away without anyone suspecting. But poor Wickham ran out of money in London and we had to stay in a small room at a tiny inn. It was cozy, but we couldn't afford to go anywhere. Then Mr. Darcy found us."

"Mr. Darcy!" Elizabeth exclaimed.

"Yes. It was all because of you," Lydia said.

"Me?"

"It seems his wife is fond of you. She told her husband that she was never as entertained as when you visited Rosings. She wanted you to be happy. She saw how upset you were and told her husband to do something."

Elizabeth looked from Lydia to Wickham in astonishment. Surely, this only confirmed that Anne Darcy had no notion of the proposal her husband made so shortly before marrying her. Elizabeth felt oddly guilty, that a woman she'd nearly superseded showed her so much kindness. She also wondered how Mr. and Mrs. Darcy found out about what happened. It was no secret in Meryton, but Elizabeth doubted that the Darcy's had corresponded with anyone who lived near Meryton.

"Yes, it's true," Wickham said.

"But I don't think I exchanged a dozen words with her at Rosings, and most of those were greetings or farewells," Elizabeth protested.

"Darcy told us she admired how you stood up to Lady Catherine," Wickham said. "I was stunned myself, and a little amused to see how Fitzwilliam Darcy of Pemberley was ordered around by his wife. We stayed two nights there on our way to Gretna Green. He may have thought he had a meek bride, but she was in charge. She negotiated everything."

Wickham's smugly amused tone sealed Elizabeth's abhorrence of him. She wondered how Mr. Darcy stood it. Letting Wickham sleep under his roof and paying for Wickham to have a good life must have been very difficult. Elizabeth couldn't understand this at all. She had a horrified thought. Was Georgiana forced to witness this? But Lydia's thoughtless prattle soon informed her that Georgiana wasn't at Pemberley. Elizabeth could legitimately ask after her when Lydia brought the subject up. Wickham told them she was visiting relatives. There was no shame in his voice, nor was there a hint that Georgiana meant anything special to him.

It was, she realized, yet another thing Anne must not know the truth of: Wickham and Georgiana. Had she, she could not possibly have asked Darcy to do as he had. Even blind to the pain she surely caused her husband, the notion of Anne Darcy ordering Mr. Darcy around was hard to fathom. Elizabeth didn't think anyone could order him around, or that Anne was the type to. Wickham, most likely, was once again taking liberties with the truth.

After Lydia and Wickham left, which wasn't soon enough for Elizabeth's liking, there was still much discussion of Elizabeth's role in bringing about the marriage. Mrs. Bennet was clearly baffled. She didn't understand how anyone could like Elizabeth so much, but Jane defended her good qualities, in her unassuming way.

Mrs. Bennet did concede that she appreciated Elizabeth helping bring about such a fine match for Lydia. She gave the Darcy's less credit for it than they deserved and Lydia received no disapproval. Mr. Bennet suggested she charm other wealthy people to marry off her sisters in reverse order of birth, since that was where she started. This pleased Kitty and Mary, not realizing Mr. Bennet gave a veiled insult, since he would prefer they leave Longbourn before Jane and Elizabeth.

Elizabeth retired as early as possible. Though her mind was too full to sleep, it was also too worn to tolerate any more time with her mother and younger sisters. She envied Anne Darcy. For the fact that she was now mistress of her own home. For the resources that allowed her to save Lydia's reputation, and shield Elizabeth and her sisters from the shame of scandal. And, she admitted as her mind finally slipped toward sleep, recalling an image of one of Darcy's rare smiles, perhaps for other things.

Chapter 5

"Of course you must go," Anne said. "Georgiana needs you."

"Our aunt is perfectly capable of handling her. My place is at your side," Darcy said. He wasn't fond of the London season, but under other circumstanced would have gone, knowing his presence would make it easier for Georgiana. He felt his duty lay in being with his pregnant wife, however, and used that truth to obscure his other reason for staying. He loved Pemberley, and had come to realize Anne did not. He found he resented his wife's indifference to his home and was loath to leave her in command of what he held so dear.

"Georgiana will be much more comfortable with you being there," Anne said. She had that note in her voice. The one he knew meant he would have no peace until he conceded. No one in his life ever argued with Darcy as Anne did. He was accustomed to people giving in to his wishes, and didn't know how to reiterate them, in the face of continued refusal, without being rude. Out of deference to her nerves, and his, he acquiesced, sending a silent apology to his cherished estate.

Anne wouldn't hurt Pemberley, he knew. She was more likely to ignore it, and his staff was capable of handling issues that she didn't bother with. Before he left, because it was the correct thing to do, he ordered Mrs. Reynolds to obey Anne, even though he trusted his housekeeper more than his wife.

Darcy realized he should be grateful that Anne didn't resent his concern about Georgiana's first season. For any faults he may see in his wife, he admitted she showed a remarkable absence of jealousy. That this lack stemmed from a complete and unassailable disregard for his affection was, perhaps, his own fault. Not for lack of trying to engage her, for he did, but for not stipulating regard as one of the contingencies on which to base their marriage before he committed to it.

Relieved to be able to turn his thoughts from Anne, he moved to contemplating the happier notion of his sister's joy when he arrived in London. He resolved to join her for every large party and even to act sociably, dancing with the wallflowers. Now that he was no longer an eligible bachelor, he knew he wouldn't be quite so welcome in London, but if he behaved well enough society would accept him. He pressed his lips into a grim line. The irony of having to turn himself into an asset at parties in order to be invited where he wanted to go was not lost on him.

Darcy continued to contemplate his new role of trying to be affable as he traveled to London, formulating a plan. Shortly before he arrived, it occurred to him that he would be criticized for not bringing his wife with him to London and he wrestled with how to spread word of her health and condition without seeming to have spoken of such untoward gossip.

This fissure in his new persona of likeability was shored, he found, before he even took action to counter it. He soon learned that any criticism of his perceived oafishness was muted by Anne. In one of her frequent bouts of thoughtfulness, which Darcy still could not reconcile with the more devious side of her nature, she wrote several of their mutual relatives that she was grateful he didn't force her to make the trip. He once again tried to muster gratitude for his wife, but in his heart he wasn't sure if he could ever resolve her daily actions with the deceit of spying on and trapping him.

When Elizabeth received the letter from Mrs. Darcy, she was filled with trepidation. Could Anne Darcy have found out that her husband proposed to Elizabeth before proposing to her? Did the carefully folded pages contain the recrimination of a woman who had shown Elizabeth nothing but kindness?

Elizabeth steeled herself to reasonableness. Even if Mr. Darcy told Anne about his failed proposal to her, an embarrassment Elizabeth couldn't see Darcy imposing upon himself, she knew Anne to be a sensible person. Elizabeth could hardly be blamed for Anne de Bourgh being Darcy's second choice, and Anne Darcy had come out ahead, hadn't she? After all, she had his regard now, and Elizabeth had nothing but the added estrangement of now being legally related to Wickham.

She opened the letter and read it, surprised at the invitation contained within. Surely, this was proof Anne still didn't know of Darcy's onetime feelings for Elizabeth. Her worry was once again replaced by guilt, though she knew herself to be blameless for Anne Darcy's ignorance. It was her husband's place, if anyone's, to tell her of the esteem he once held Elizabeth in. Still, she felt it would be dishonest, accepting kindness from a woman who had justifiable reason for keeping her at arm's length.

29

Yet, she felt a strong pull toward Pemberley. She knew that draw to be only partially because of the beauty of Pemberley and partially because it was his home. No good could come of being there, with the very essence of Mr. Darcy all around her. Yet, he would be safely in London.

Unsure at her own feelings, let alone what response to give, she resolved to read the letter to her parents at dinner. Later, at the table, it took Elizabeth some time to break through the incessant chatter of her mother, Mary and Kitty, but once the author of the letter she held was revealed, all fell into eager silence. Holding the letter before her, Elizabeth read:

Dear Miss Bennet,
I would love to have you visit me at Pemberley. Mr. Darcy and Miss Darcy will be in London for the season, since she is coming out. My indifferent health does not allow me to participate in this. While I prefer the comforts of Pemberley to the bustle of London, I find it lonely. Please allow me to send a carriage and a maid to escort you to Pemberley....

"Of course you must go," said Mrs. Bennet, breaking into Elizabeth's reading. "She might introduce you to some eligible young men."

"After your trip to Kent and your tour with the Gardiners, I am aware of how much I will miss you," Mr. Bennet said. "However, considering what she did for Lydia, you really must go."

"You really must," Jane murmured. "Though I shall miss you, too."

Elizabeth took Jane's hand. Since returning from her tour she'd grown increasingly worried about her older sister. Jane was quiet, even for her, and spent much of her time holding a book or embroidery, but doing nothing. Elizabeth was sure her sister was still brokenhearted. Maybe, if she went, she could tell Mrs. Darcy just that small detail of her interactions with Mr. Darcy. Just enough to enlist Anne's aid in bringing Jane and Mr. Bingley together.

"What else did she say?" Mary demanded, looking a bit envious.

Mrs. Darcy warned Elizabeth to bring warm clothing and gave more details about her journey. At her mother's urging, Elizabeth wrote her acceptance. She spent the intervening time packing, but found she had no other details to attend to. The middle aged woman who came with the carriage arranged everything.

When she arrived at Pemberley, after a long journey made no easier by her companion's taciturn nature and her own nervousness about the wisdom of her decision to come, Anne Darcy greeted her at the door. To Elizabeth's shock, Mrs. Darcy was visibly pregnant. Though she was sure she bore no strong feelings for Mr. Darcy, and knew him to be a happily married man, Elizabeth was taken aback by such formidable evidence of his marital contentment.

Fortunately, as she was rendered speechless by how fully unprepared she was for Mrs. Darcy's condition, Elizabeth was saved by Anne's warm greeting. Elizabeth realized she'd assumed, when Mrs. Darcy cited her health as reason for not going to London, that it was no more than the ongoing frailness of her constitution. It was disconcerting that Mrs. Darcy hadn't mentioned her gravid condition. She continued in that vein, to Elizabeth's growing discomfort, until after dinner.

"You may wonder that Mr. Darcy isn't here for my pregnancy," she said.

Elizabeth shook her head. Although she did not think Mr. Darcy would ignore any responsibility, many men gave their wives no special attention during pregnancy.

"I didn't want Georgiana to be deprived of her season because of something she had no control over, and I knew having her brother absent would inhibit the poor dear to the point of deprivation. I missed my chance at a season because of the death of my father, and was never well enough to have one later."

"I'm sorry," Elizabeth said, unable to think of anything else to say. She was, she found, still nervous in Mrs. Darcy's company, feeling as she did, like she carried a grave secret. She was also a bit startled both by how forthcoming her hostess was and her uncharacteristic verbosity. Married life must agree with Mrs. Darcy as well.

"My aunt, Colonel Fitzwilliam's mother, is bringing out her youngest daughter. Georgiana will share in all the activities. Georgiana is more comfortable with people she knows, which should make the season easier for her. If she doesn't find a husband this season, she can have another season next year. By then, she should be more confident about London and will be fine without her cousin. Next year, I hope I will be well enough to join her in London and offer guidance of my own, such as it will be."

"Under the circumstances, I'm surprised Mr. Darcy feels he needs to be there," Elizabeth said. Realizing her words may be taken as criticism, she hastened to add. "I was under the impression he was not fond of parties."

Mrs. Darcy smiled at this. "He hates them. But Miss Darcy fears them, and my husband will always do his duty to those he feels responsible for. I don't need him here, I need a woman friend."

"I would have thought..." Elizabeth broke off, not wanting to suggest that Mrs. Darcy should have a friend who was closer to her. She obviously didn't. Recovering, she said, "Wouldn't Mrs. Jenkinson be a better choice than me?"

"No. She was my mother's choice, not mine. I hoped to make friends with Mrs. Collins, but it's clear that she cannot leave her husband alone for long. He isn't competent enough to manage by himself. If work is done in the parish, she does it. She's a remarkable woman. I was delighted when she moved in. Unfortunately, my mother kept me from making friends with anyone. She thought having a companion was enough. But Mrs. Jenkinson was loyal to my mother, not me."

"How unfortunate," Elizabeth said. Though she was pleased by the praise of Charlotte, she was still taken aback by Mrs. Darcy's forthrightness. She never thought she would pity someone with great wealth, but she pitied Anne Darcy. She lived a very constricted life. Perhaps her inviting someone as far beneath her as Elizabeth was a rebellion, of sorts.

"Yes, it was. Because of that, I want you to promise me something. I'm so sick of people reporting to my mother behind my back. If I didn't eat my breakfast, my mother would know it. I don't want that here."

"That's understandable," Elizabeth said, her pity for Anne growing. "What do you want me to promise you?"

"That you won't write my mother or Mr. Darcy about me, no matter what happens. That is, unless I die. Then someone will have to write them."

"That's an easy promise to keep," Elizabeth said, unsuccessfully trying to ignore the morbid nature of Mrs. Darcy's statement. She knew Mrs. Darcy's health was poor, but it seemed ill omened to speak so openly about such a terrible eventuality. "I wouldn't presume to write either Mr. Darcy or your mother." She wasn't on terms with Lady Catherine to write her. As for Mr. Darcy, how could she write him about anything?

"You promise?" Anne asked, eerily intent.

"Yes, of course."

Chapter 6

Mrs. Darcy planned for Elizabeth's entertainment. Once or twice a week, a local family was invited to Pemberley to dinner. Mrs. Darcy found the trip to neighboring estates too much to cope with, and she explained she didn't like large parties. She preferred the more intimate nature of a smaller gathering where she could observe and listen to all that went on. Not long after each dinner, Mrs. Darcy would plead fatigue and retire. Most families would take that as their cue to depart, to Elizabeth's relief. She didn't want to be responsible for entertaining their guests alone. On two occasions, there were eligible young men, and they were seated next to Elizabeth, but in those short acquaintance all she achieved was pleasant conversation for the evening, not anything resembling courtship.

Since Mrs. Darcy slept every afternoon, Elizabeth filled her time with long walks about the magnificent grounds and the countryside beyond, and hours of indulging in selecting new books to read in Pemberley's extensive library. If the weather was particularly nice, Mrs. Darcy took Elizabeth on a carriage ride, usually just around Pemberley. Once, they went to Lambton to visit the wet nurse Mrs. Darcy planned to use, a broad-faced, complacent woman with a toddler.

They attended church every Sunday. Elizabeth enjoyed listening to a different clergyman. Reverend Barton, a pleasant man in his thirties, was a gifted speaker. His sermons suggested a stricter morality than the laissez fair attitude of the Meryton sermons but lacked the antagonizing sanctimoniousness of Mr. Collins'. Elizabeth briefly wondered if Lydia would have benefited from Reverend Barton's sermons. Probably not, since she and Kitty rarely listened in Meryton. Certainly, though, Jane and Mary would appreciate them.

As the days passed, Elizabeth grew more comfortable in Mrs. Darcy's company. She no longer had to remind herself that it wasn't her place to tell Mrs. Darcy anything, for she stopped thinking of Darcy's proposal to her as some grave secret. It was obvious that Mr. and Mrs. Darcy were quite happy, relegating Elizabeth's place in his affections firmly and unalterably in the past. Where, she told herself, it unequivocally belonged.

On one of her afternoon walks, Elizabeth passed a tenant

cottage where a woman was getting firewood from a well-stocked woodpile. The woman was heavily pregnant, further along than Mrs. Darcy. Feeling she shouldn't be straining herself, Elizabeth asked, "Can I help you carry some of that?"

"You're visiting the manor house?" The woman asked. Elizabeth nodded. "You'll dirty your clothes, miss."

"I'm more concerned about you carrying so much." Elizabeth picked up a load of wood, knowing the laundress at Pemberley would attend to any dirt. There was no firewood in the cottage, causing Elizabeth to take enough trips to fill the space reserved for it. "Can't your husband do this?" Elizabeth asked.

"Nay," the woman said. "My husband died two months ago. My son is out shoring up the road. He'll want a good meal when he comes home." The woman offered her tea, which Elizabeth declined, knowing the price of tea could take a toll on a tenant farmer's income.

Elizabeth claimed to be tired, though she wasn't, and asked to sit down and rest a while. Familiar with the pride of country folk, she wanted to allow the cottager to do something for her, in return for her labor. The cottager introduced herself as Nelly Douglas. She was very eager to have someone to talk to. Her son was seventeen and doing a man's work. The son was trying to earn a little extra money before the baby was born. Within a very short time, Nelly told Elizabeth a great deal about her situation. Her two daughters were knee deep in their own children. One was in Lambton and the other nearby on another tenant farm.

At dinner that evening, Mrs. Darcy asked her, as was her custom, "How was your walk?"

"Enjoyable. I met one of your tenants, a woman named Nelly Douglas. She is very pregnant, widowed, and alone all day. I'm concerned if she goes into labor, she'll have no one near to help her." Elizabeth chose her phrasing carefully, trying not to sound as if she were presuming to advise Anne, who was, after all, mistress of Pemberley.

"Do you think I should do something?" Anne gratified Elizabeth by asking.

"I don't know if it's your responsibility or that of your steward," Elizabeth said, still unwilling to overstep.

"I'll inquire."

Anne found her steward was aware of the situation, as she'd assumed he would be. One of the things she enjoyed about being mistress of Pemberley was that it all but ran itself. She needn't concern herself with any details she didn't take an interest in, and those were quite few. Darcy handled everything or had someone who did.

To reassure Elizabeth, Anne informed her that Nelly Douglas was checked on a couple of times a day and arrangements were already made for a neighbor to stay with her after the baby was born. They knew about the son's absence, since it was a project sponsored by Pemberley to keep the road open between Pemberley and Lambton. She explained this to Elizabeth, who asked tentatively, "Is it the custom here to arrange gifts for the new baby?"

"I'm not certain," Anne said. "But what would she need? Our steward said this is her eleventh child, although only three lived to adulthood. Most died as babies. Surely, there are enough baby clothes and diapers." Anne couldn't fathom being with child eleven times, nor want to think about babies dying. She allowed her tone to be a bit abrupt, hoping Elizabeth would select another topic.

"Those might be used by her grandchildren." That hadn't occurred to Anne. It was obvious Elizabeth knew much more about these things than she did. "Longbourn is a smaller, much less elegant place," Elizabeth continued. "We give our tenants both clothing and food, but we didn't have nearly as many tenants as are at Pemberley. It's easier to know all of them."

Anne reached for a bell and rang it. She appreciated Elizabeth's attempt at tact, but realized she didn't know any of the tenants here. She knew many at Rosings, but even there she wouldn't know what was sent on such an occasion. At Rosings, her mother had prevented her from involvement in things. Here, she simply hadn't taken the effort.

When a maid responded, Anne asked for Mrs. Reynolds to be sent for. "I'll ask her," Anne said, a little embarrassed she couldn't answer the question herself. It occurred to her that if Elizabeth had married Darcy, she would know by now. Anne didn't like the comparison, and quickly pressed it from her mind. Elizabeth was to be her friend, not her rival. She, after all, had Darcy as her husband. Nothing could ever change that.

Mrs. Reynolds came promptly, nodding as Anne reiterated Elizabeth's question. Mrs. Reynolds told them, "Mr. Darcy said to continue with past custom concerning these things."

Anne appreciated Mrs. Reynolds' tact as well, but felt her face color slightly. She could almost hear the housekeep add, 'So as not to trouble you, ma'am.' She realized Mrs. Reynolds was still speaking, detailing the food and fabric that Pemberley gave for each birth, and endeavored to pay attention.

"Considering Miss Bennet's interest, would it be appropriate to augment this?" Anne asked when the list was finished.

"Certainly, especially considering Mrs. Douglas' recent widowhood."

Anne watched as Elizabeth and Mrs. Reynolds discussed what should be done, a bit envious at the easy interaction between the two women and Elizabeth's obvious knowledge of what was needed. In particular, Elizabeth mentioned they needed to be sure that Mrs. Douglas had plenty of firewood in her cottage at all times.

Anne was unsure why that was so important to Elizabeth, but as she watched Darcy's first love take charge of something that should be her duty, a plan began to form in her mind. Anne had no illusions about her health. She'd made provisions for Rosings to go to her child. It was her duty to make provisions for Pemberley and Darcy as well. Darcy wasn't the only one who knew what duty was. She didn't know how yet, but Anne would find a means of keep Elizabeth at Pemberley, should she die.

Seeking a way to contribute to the conversation at hand, Anne suggested that she and Elizabeth could make a few additional items for Mrs. Douglas' baby, recalling that was one thing she had done at Rosings. It would be a good use of her time, she felt, and she already had an ample supply of baby clothes for her own child. In fact, with so much time at her disposal and unlimited resources, she already had clothing to last the first year and beyond.

When that project commenced the following day, Anne found it particularly pleasing, since she sewed better than Elizabeth. She hid her satisfaction in finding one area which she excelled in, while they both worked on a layette for the impending Douglas baby. Elizabeth further bolstered her ego by being generous with her praise.

Anne enjoyed making garments for her own child but never thought of doing it for anyone else at Pemberley. It gave her a sense of satisfaction to do something useful. Mrs. Jenkinson had encouraged her to sew charitable garments for Rosings' tenants' children, but that had been an abstract idea, with Mrs. Jenkinson advising her on what fabrics to use and what size garments to make. Somehow, it meant more when it was her own choices and her own idea.

Two weeks later, they took the carriage to deliver the layette. Anne was surprised at how well kept the cottage was, considering the exceedingly gravid state of Mrs. Douglas. She was also surprised at the spaciousness of the dwelling and the quality of the furnishings. If this was typical, the tenants here had better housing than those at Rosings. Anne wondered if that meant Darcy was overly generous, but rather suspected her mother was overly stingy. She wondered if she should make an effort to change things at Rosings.

Elizabeth came into the parlor one day and found Mrs. Darcy embroidering. It looked like another baby garment, but Mrs. Darcy had more than enough embroidered garments and they weren't embroidering clothing for the Douglas baby. Of course, Anne seemed to enjoy doing it and had a very fine stitch, so she was most likely doing it for her own enjoyment. Mrs. Darcy folded the garment and put it in the basket by her chair, saying, "I want to show you something."

Elizabeth waited while Anne arose. Mrs. Darcy was wrapped in shawls and blankets and it took her a while to shed them. She led Elizabeth up a flight of stairs and down a corridor, opening the door to a beautiful bedroom. It was a woman's room with simple, yet elegant, furniture. The furniture was in a light wood and the bed hangings were a pale green. The green and the light wood were echoed throughout the room, with two exceptions. There was a chaise lounge which was more ornate than Pemberley's furniture but at least looked comfortable. There also was a dark wood desk which didn't fit the carefully planned décor. It had elaborate carvings all over it. It stood out, in an unfortunate way. The handles to the drawers and cabinets had flowers on them, which echoed carved wooden flowers all over the desk. It didn't look right in the room. It might not look right anywhere.

"This is my room," Mrs. Darcy said. "Mr. Darcy said I could redecorate it, but I like his mother's tastes. The curtains and bed hangings needed replacing, but I copied the ones that were here."

"It's very nice," Elizabeth said, eying the desk, hoping Mrs. Darcy would not ask her to comment on it.

"The desk is hideous," Mrs. Darcy said, a smile curving her lips. "I obviously brought it from Rosings."

"If it's hideous, why did you bring it?" Elizabeth asked, surprised by Anne's ready admission.

"Because it was my grandmother's."

"Were you close to your grandmother?"

"I was close to both of them," Anne said, gazing past Elizabeth, out the window. Her face took on a wistful continence that Elizabeth was learning to recognize as Anne recalling the time in her life before she grew ill. "This was the Countess' desk. She was my maternal grandmother. She was the one who taught my mother that the more sumptuous and ornate something is, the better it looks. Thus, Rosings as you see it today. But she read me stories and listened to my childish prattle. I loved her." Anne smiled again, turning to face Elizabeth as she continued. "My father's mother taught me to embroider. She also taught me practical sewing. My mother said there was no reason for me to know how to sew my own clothes or to make baby clothes, but I'm glad I learned. The nice thing about sewing is that I can work at it for a few minutes and put it down. When I come back, it's still there, whether it be a minute later or a month later. I give a few things to the poor every year. Not a lot. But if a family gets a baby gown from me, they might remember me." This last was spoken with a melancholy that gave Elizabeth pause, for she'd never heard Anne sound so sad before.

"That's nice of you," Elizabeth said, deciding to respond to the words, rather than the tone.

"I also like the desk because it has a secret compartment, just like in the tales my grandmother used to read me. I'm fascinated by how well constructed it is, in spite of its garishness. Let me show you."

"Oh no," Elizabeth said, raising a hand in protest. "I wouldn't want to intrude."

This time, Elizabeth found Anne's smile inscrutable. Ignoring her protests, Mrs. Darcy moved to the desk. "Watch," she said, proceeding to adjust a wooden lily, an iris and a daffodil. When all three carved flowers were moved, there was a small slot visible, which could be used to open a compartment. "Open the 'lid,' grandmamma said. That's how I should remember the flowers. L for lily, I for iris and D for daffodil. Here, you try."

Still feeling intrusive, but fascinated by the craftsmanship, Elizabeth complied. She was surprised at how easy it was. Several other flowers moved, but didn't appear to open anything. "You have nothing in the compartment," she said, opening and closing the lid as she tried to spy the invisible mechanisms that made the compartment work.

"That's because I have nothing I need to hide," Anne said with that same unreadable smile.

Elizabeth felt a pang of regret. She had to hide Mr. Darcy's proposal and her growing feeling that it was a mistake to refuse him. That was a horrible thought, considering he was married, and worse yet, married to her hostess.

Wouldn't it be nice to have nothing to hide?

38

Chapter 7

Elizabeth was sorry that the next several days were too wet to walk. After one day spent almost entirely reading, and a second at quietly practicing on Georgiana's beautiful pianoforte, she ended up pacing the halls of Pemberley. It didn't quite satisfy her longing for exercise, since there was something about being outdoors which she needed. To make matters worse, a servant on horseback cancelled a local family's coming to dinner, citing bad roads. Elizabeth realized her only real company here was Mrs. Darcy, who was spending an increasing amount of time in her bedroom or the adjoining sitting room.

When word came that Nelly Douglas delivered a healthy boy, Elizabeth decided she had to visit. She asked Mrs. Reynolds to prepare a basket of food and borrowed an umbrella. Even though she knew it showed a lack of decorum, she paced the foyer until the rain subsided to a mere drizzle, then took the opportunity to make a dash to Nelly's cottage.

She was pleased when a neighbor answered the door, having feared the rain would inhibit the help Mrs. Reynolds told her Nelly would receive. After admiring the baby and delivering the food, she saw the drizzle was turning into a loud patter and the wind was picking up. Concerned conditions outside would only worsen, she bid a hasty farewell and left. It quickly became clear the wind was too strong for the use of an umbrella, making the device into more of a liability than an asset. She closed it and started running. She arrived muddy and soaking wet.

When dressed in dry clothing, she rushed to put up her still-damp hair in preparation for dinner. She arrived in the dining room exactly on the hour, a bit flustered from her hurry, only to be told that Mrs. Darcy wasn't coming down. Elizabeth ate her dinner in solitary state, wishing she dared read at the table. She finished quickly and escaped to the library to select something with which to entertain herself for the rest of the evening.

The next morning, she resolved to check on Mrs. Darcy. Even if she was not allowed to write to Lady Catharine, if Mrs. Darcy was less well than usual, there must be something Elizabeth could do. She walked down corridor, spotting a maid leaving Mrs. Darcy's room. She was chewing, but stopped upon seeing Elizabeth.

"Is Mrs. Darcy up to seeing visitors?" Elizabeth asked.

"Yes, Ma'am." The girl said, her garbled words betraying the food in her mouth.

"Thank you." Elizabeth knocked and was bid enter.

Mrs. Darcy was sitting, with her feet up, in an ornate chaise lounge matching the one Elizabeth saw in her bed chamber the day Anne showed her the desk. Looking around, Elizabeth could see that nothing else in this room was from Rosings. Aside from the chase, everything had the clean elegant lines of Pemberley. The chaises must be very comfortable indeed, Elizabeth reflected, for Anne to bring them when she obviously preferred Mr. Darcy's style to her mother's.

"Good morning, Mrs. Darcy," Elizabeth said. "I hope I'm not disturbing you?"

"Of course not," Anne said. She gestured to a nearby chair. "Please, sit."

"I was concerned about you, since you didn't come down for dinner." Elizabeth said, seating herself.

"I wasn't feeling well, but you see I'm better. I've eaten my breakfast."

The empty plate suggested someone ate it, but Elizabeth doubted it was Mrs. Darcy. She was doubly sad for Mrs. Darcy, both because she wasn't eating and because she was so terrified of being spied on that she engaged in such subterfuge. Always thin, she looked tinnier than before, in spite of her pregnancy. Elizabeth wished she could consult someone about her hostess' health, but didn't know anyone near to consult.

Feeling it her only means of helping Mrs. Darcy in any way, Elizabeth resolved to play her part as companion as best she could. She ignored the empty plate and talked cheerfully about Nelly Douglas. She spoke of the cottager's easy delivery, and her healthy son, being sure not to mention any of the less savory rigors of childbirth.

"She named him Fitz in honor of Mr. Darcy. I hope you don't mind," Elizabeth said. She elected not tell Mrs. Darcy that Fitz' middle name was Bennet, because Nelly recognized some of the help she received from Pemberley came from Elizabeth.

"Of course not. I'm sure my husband will be pleased," Mrs. Darcy said. She sounded as tired as she looked.

"Mrs. Darcy," Elizabeth said, causing Anne to open eyes

which had sunk shut. "Is there anything you need? Something or someone I can send for?"

"I simply need to rest," Mrs. Darcy said. "Thank you for entertaining me." She gave Elizabeth a warm smile. "I do appreciate how trying so much solitude must be for you, who have four sisters and both mother and father. It's good of you to stay on."

"It's not kindness," Elizabeth said, wanting to give solace to this woman, who seemed to have everything and yet had so little. "I am your friend. I'll stay here until you are well or Mr. Darcy returns."

Mrs. Darcy smiled, but even such a small act seemed to cause her effort. "On such kind words, I think I shall take a nap. Please forgive my dismissal."

Elizabeth stood. "Send for me if you need me," she said, but Mrs. Darcy's eyes were already closed.

Hurrying from the room with light steps, Elizabeth immediately sought Mrs. Reynolds, who was in the kitchen overseeing the inventorying of the spices. Elizabeth didn't like to interrupt, but Mrs. Darcy's increased pallor and weakness concerned her deeply. "Mrs. Reynolds, may I trouble you for a moment aside?"

The housekeeper nodded, setting down her ledger and leading Elizabeth to a quiet room off of the kitchen. "Yes, Miss Bennet?"

"I'm worried about Mrs. Darcy's health," Elizabeth said, feeling no need to mince her words with Mrs. Reynolds. "I don't know anyone to consult on this. I can't write Mr. Darcy. Could you do so?"

"Mr. Darcy told me to follow Mrs. Darcy's orders and she ordered me not to write him about her health. She even told him she would do that and he reinforced her order."

Elizabeth was surprised at this, wondering if Wickham was correct when he said that Mrs. Darcy ordered Mr. Darcy about. He must truly be besotted with her. It was not, then, a union born solely of convenience.

"I promised not to write Mr. Darcy or her mother," Elizabeth admitted, pacing the small room. Suddenly, she had an idea. Her friend, Mrs. Collins, saw Mrs. Darcy's mother regularly. "But there is someone I can write," she said, halting her steps to turn to Mrs. Reynolds.

"Do so soon or the roads will be impassable in this rain," Mrs. Reynolds said, her usually calm tone tinged with urgency and hope.

Elizabeth hurried to her room to compose the letter. She wrote quickly, describing the situation and her concern, making sure Charlotte knew that Mr. Darcy hasn't been informed for no one at

Pemberley had the means to write him. Elizabeth knew she was breaking the spirit of her promise, but surely someone should be informed about Mrs. Darcy's health. When she returned downstairs, Mrs. Reynolds had a rider waiting, to ensure the letter caught the mail.

On his return, the mud spattered rider reported success in his mission, but that the roads were impassable to carriages. He said most of the tenants were pulled from other employments to attempt to shore them up, but he didn't think even that would help for long. His news brought new worries to Elizabeth, both that it was too late to summon help for Mrs. Darcy and that Nelly Douglas and her new baby would be neglected. She didn't wish for Nelly to lose yet another child.

That afternoon, Elizabeth had her dinner in Mrs. Darcy's room and gently bullied her into eating. She kept an eagle-eye on her hostess' plate, worried that Mrs. Darcy would sneak away food, and watched until almost half of the content of each dish was consumed. As much of her focus as that took, there was another issue Elizabeth felt she should attend to.

"I'm concerned about Nelly Douglas and Fitz," she said, hoping to distract Mrs. Darcy almost as much as she hoped to help the cottager and her child. "I was told that the rains have created more work for the men and some of the women are working, too. Would it be too much to ask to have Nelly and her baby come to Pemberley?"

"Of course not," Mrs. Darcy said.

To Elizabeth's satisfaction, the topic seemed to stir a small level of energy in Mrs. Darcy. She reached for the pull cord that rang for a servant, but when the girl arrived, her orders were to accept Miss Bennet's orders on this issue. While she was pleased to be allowed to conduct the move as she liked, she'd hoped Mrs. Darcy's interest in Nelly and Fitz would stir her to a slightly more active role. Mrs. Darcy's increased listlessness concerned Elizabeth deeply.

The following morning, Elizabeth consulted Mrs. Darcy's coachman, who told her a carriage trip was longer and risked being caught in the mud. He seemed nervous as he said it, as if fearing she would blame him for the state of the roads. Assuring him she understood there was only so much a carriage could accomplish, Elizabeth sought out Mrs. Reynolds for help.

In the end, it was agreed Elizabeth would bring four men with her to help the move. Before leaving the manor, Elizabeth made it clear that Nelly and Fitz were to have a room with a fireplace, meaning it must be a guest bedroom. She also ordered a hot bath drawn, knowing Mrs. Douglas would be wet and cold by the time they returned. Before she made the request, Elizabeth worried Mrs. Reynolds would protest such breaches of protocol, but the housekeeper seemed pleased.

Thanking her, Elizabeth tied her hat tightly in place and went out to meet the men Mrs. Reynolds sent for. As they came from working on the roads, the men were already soaked through. They slogged through the rain, following Elizabeth to the cottage. She didn't wait for a break in the weather this time, as an end to the storm wasn't in sight. When they arrived, Nelly's voice answered Elizabeth's knock, bidding them enter. She was disappointed, but not surprised, to find Nelly and Fitz in the cottage alone, the fire burned low and no one about to help them.

Nelly Douglas listened to Elizabeth's offer, gratitude blooming on her face, and accepted readily. Thought still weak from childbirth, Nelly was able to walk, especially since a strong man held each arm. Elizabeth carried the baby while another man held an umbrella over them. The fourth carried those things that Nelly felt she would need. They moved slowly, but they arrived at Pemberley safely, where the requested guest bedroom and hot bath were ready for Nelly. Fitz was changed into dry clothing and a maid sat with him by the fire until Nelly was ready to hold him. The cottager looked exhausted, causing Elizabeth to fret that she'd done more harm than good by bringing her.

This fear grew into self-recrimination as the rain became more intermittent. Elizabeth realized she may have made the choice to bring Nelly to Pemberley too hastily, and certainly should have waited to see if the storm let up before dragging the poor woman and her child through the rain. She was consoled by learning that the rain, though no longer a constant downpour, still continued often enough so there was concern about the roads, keeping workers much too busy to give Nelly and Fitz the assistance they would be counting on.

As one rainy day melded into another, and Elizabeth found it increasingly difficult to badger Mrs. Darcy into eating, or even keep her awake, she began to fear her letter must not have gotten through. Surely, Lady Catherine must have set out the moment she read of her daughter's condition. Mr. Darcy, too, should be returned, as his mother-in-law would have informed him of the information Elizabeth gave her. Her elaboration to Charlotte that Mr. Darcy didn't know was, after all, as close as she could come to requesting Lady Catherine write him.

Elizabeth's concerns turned out to be unnecessary, at least in the case of Lady Catherine. Mrs. Darcy's mother arrived the very afternoon Elizabeth resolved to compose a second letter, filling the manor with her imperiousness in an instant. She was trailed into Pemberley by a stout stern-looking woman who Lady Catherine declared to be the finest midwife in England. Leveling her haughty gaze on Elizabeth, Lady Catherine said, "In case no one here has the wits or experience to help my daughter."

Elizabeth wasn't blind to the insult, but was too relieved to have help for Mrs. Darcy to protest. Indeed, it was only a partially unjust accusation. Elizabeth felt she possessed plenty of wit, and some modicum of experience, but not enough to help Mrs. Darcy.

Lady Catherine's arrival with the midwife was timely, for Mrs. Darcy went into labor that very evening. Elizabeth spent the night pacing the hall outside Mrs. Darcy's room, for Lady Catherine wouldn't permit her to enter. The next morning, well after Elizabeth refused Mrs. Reynolds' offer of breakfast, the midwife stepped into the hall, softly closing the door behind her.

"The baby is here," she said. "It's a girl. Mrs. Darcy is very weak. I can't advise that she nurse the child. Once I've cleaned her, I'll bring her out and you can take her to the wet nurse."

"But she's in Lambton," Elizabeth said. She hadn't meant to raise her voice, but fatigue and worry were taking their toll. "We sent for her immediately, but I don't know if word can even get through, let alone anyone return with her."

With a look that clearly admonished Elizabeth's tone, the midwife slipped back into Mrs. Darcy's room, closing the door before Elizabeth could even glimpse her. A moment later, Lady Catherine stepped out. Her expression made it clear she'd rather be wiping a bug off the bottom of her shoe than speaking to Elizabeth.

"In the future, Miss Bennet, you shall remember that you are in my daughter's home, where you have no right to raise your voice nor countermand my orders."

"I beg your pardon, Lady Catherine," Elizabeth said, truly contrite for speaking loudly enough for Mrs. Darcy to hear. "I didn't mean to disturb Mrs. Darcy or to ignore your request for the wet nurse. She's been sent for, but it's impossible to say if word can even reach her and I doubt there's any chance of her arrival until the roads are more passable."

"You will have to do the best you can, Miss Bennet, for I won't have my daughter weakened further by nursing a child, especially one who is too small to survive."

Before Elizabeth could press aside her shock to formulate a

reply, Lady Catherine reentered Mrs. Darcy's room. Elizabeth stood before the door, trying to decide if she should risk agitating Mrs. Darcy by knocking, or simply barge in. She couldn't allow Lady Catherine to decide for Mrs. Darcy if her child was worth feeding. The woman was monstrous. Surely, Elizabeth owned it to Mrs. Darcy to seek her preference in the matter.

Before she could come to a decision, the midwife returned, holding out a poorly wrapped squirming bundle. The first thing Elizabeth noticed was that the child was terribly small. The second, that her cries were pitifully weak. The third was that she had six toes on each foot. It seemed odd, but when Elizabeth opened her mouth to comment on it, the midwife thrust the baby at her saying, "I don't know if there's anything to be done for her, but she can't stay. She'll only distress the patient." Shaking her head, the woman disappeared into the room.

Elizabeth cradled the tiny form with care. She adjusted the blanket, the stitching on it obviously Mrs. Darcy's careful work, swaddling the baby as best she could while holding her. She'd never beheld anything so fragile and so in need of help. She wondered if they even let Mrs. Darcy hold her once. Casting a last look at the door, torn between helping Mrs. Darcy's baby and worrying that Mrs. Darcy needed help too, locked away under Lady Catherine's care as she was, Elizabeth hurried off to find Mrs. Douglas.

Nelly was awake and sitting in her chair. She was of a hearty stock, and looked well, but Elizabeth knew she still tired quiet easily. Yet, the tiny baby needed milk, and she didn't look as if she'd be much of a burden on Nelly. Elizabeth crossed the room, carefully handing over her bundle.

"Nelly, would you be willing to act as wet nurse?" Elizabeth asked. "Mrs. Darcy isn't well enough and we can't reach her wet nurse in Lambton. Will it be too much for you?"

Nelly was willing, but nursed the baby only briefly before the baby slept. Elizabeth took her back. Mrs. Darcy's daughter hadn't consumed much. Compared with Fitz Douglas, the new baby seemed even tinier than she first appeared.

Having nowhere to put the baby, Elizabeth carried her with her, seeking Mrs. Reynolds. They arranged for a second cradle to be put in with Nelly, and Elizabeth settled the child into it. A little over an hour later, when she went to the door to check on them, she was surprised to hear faint cries from the new baby. "Why aren't you nursing her yet?" Elizabeth asked, entering the room.

"When she's really hungry, she'll cry," Nelly responded.

Elizabeth was appalled by her tone, both neutral and taciturn.

Thinking back, she recalled that while Nelly took proper care of Fitz, she wasn't overly solicitous of him. Was this why the woman had lost so many babies, or the result of coming to terms with it? The new baby stopped fussing and fell asleep, but Elizabeth wasn't satisfied. She couldn't believe Mrs. Darcy's baby received enough food in the first meal to satisfy her.

Crossing to the crib, treading carefully so as not to wake the sleeping Fitz, Elizabeth picked up Mrs. Darcy's baby and brought her over to Nelly. "Nurse her," she ordered. She knew she was being both presumptuous and rude, but she was exhausted and at her wits end. Didn't anyone care about Mr. and Mrs. Darcy's baby?

Nelly looked startled at the command, but she shrugged and accepted the baby. Elizabeth seated herself on the edge of the bed, waiting to make sure Mrs. Darcy's child was properly fed. It was a repeat of the previous time, with the baby only nursing for about five minutes. Nelly handed her back, her look tinged with reproach, and rose to check on her son.

Checking on them repeatedly the next day, Elizabeth found that Nelly often slept through the faint cries of Mrs. Darcy's baby but was awakened by the lusty cries of her own son. Nelly, along with everyone else, told Elizabeth Mrs. Darcy's baby was too small to live. The information was imparted to her with varying degrees of sympathy, depending on who spoke, but everyone seemed agreed on the fact. Most of the concern of the household was on Mrs. Darcy and how they could help her. Elizabeth had the cradle moved to her bedroom, since she felt she was more reliable in seeing the baby was fed than Nelly.

Mrs. Darcy must have recovered slightly, for she sent a maid, asking for her baby to be brought. Elizabeth was pleased on several counts. Mrs. Darcy, at least, seemed to care for her child and was recovering her strength, and Elizabeth would finally get to see her friend, no matter what Lady Catherine said. Carefully bundling the infant, she hastened to Mrs. Darcy's room.

Anne was propped up by pillows and smiled upon seeing the baby. The fire was burning so brightly in the room that it was overheated. Elizabeth removed the blanket she carried the baby in and placed her in Mrs. Darcy's arms. Mrs. Darcy tugged up the gown, which was too big for the baby. Elizabeth worried at Mrs. Darcy's reaction to the six toes, but when she saw them, she smiled. "She has my toes."

"Your toes?"

"I've always hated them. Darcy pretends he doesn't notice."

46

She tried to kick the blankets off her feet, but it was too much. She slipped her foot under the blanket on the side of the bed where Elizabeth was standing. Seeing her bare foot, Elizabeth saw that Mrs. Darcy did indeed have six toes.

The baby slept in her mother's lap and after a few minutes, Mrs. Darcy slept as well. Elizabeth picked up the baby, who started crying, but not loudly enough to wake her mother. Elizabeth brought her to Nelly, hoping she would eat more.

Elizabeth's world dissolved into a fog of caring for Anne's child. She found she would awaken at the slightest sound from the baby, even though the noise of the rain and the servants moving in the house didn't bother her. It frightened Elizabeth that the baby seemed to lose weight at first, and upset her that no one, not even Nelly, seemed to feel it was worth loving the child. Sometimes, when the whole of the house slept and only Elizabeth was awake, rocking the tiny infant by the fire, she felt as powerless as the baby, and tears would slide unchecked down her cheeks.

After a grueling eight days, Elizabeth began to see changes in the baby. She seemed stronger and healthier. Her cry was louder and she ate more, and slept longer. Where once she had felt duty, and then love, Elizabeth at last began to feel hope.

Mrs. Darcy asked to see her child again, and Elizabeth let her hope for the baby spill over into hope for the baby's mother. She realized she hadn't had the presence of mind to try to see her friend. That Lady Catherine, along with the rest of the household, was doing everything possible for Anne, Elizabeth was sure, for it was all anyone in the manor spoke of. Her heart lighter than it had been in days, Elizabeth brought the baby to see Mrs. Darcy.

Upon entering the room, she had to work to hide her disappointment and shock. Mrs. Darcy was thin to the point of emaciation, her skin a nearly translucent façade stretched over bone. She raised a skeletal hand, which trembled with the effort. Elizabeth realized Mrs. Darcy hadn't asked to see her baby again because she was recovering, but because she knew she approached her last moments on earth.

"Please, Elizabeth," Mrs. Darcy said, her voice a whisper. "May I hold her again?"

"Of course," Elizabeth said. She crossed the room, but didn't hand Mrs. Darcy the baby. Instead, she tucked the infant beside her, being careful not to pull the blankets too tightly over either form. As she moved to straighten, Mrs. Darcy clutched at her arm.

"You must care for her, Miss Bennet," Mrs. Darcy whispered. Her eyes, the only part of her that still seemed alive, darted about the room. "Don't let mother take her. She must stay here with Mr. Darcy. I know you are the only one I can trust with this. Please, Elizabeth, promise me you'll look after my baby. Promise me you will try to love her."

"Yes, of course, Mrs. Darcy," Elizabeth said. The hand on her arm clawed at her, demanding. "I promise. I promise that I already love her and that I'll try to see she stays here, with her father."

Saying it made Elizabeth think of him, which she hadn't had the presence of mind to do in days. Where was Mr. Darcy? He should be there. It shouldn't be up to Elizabeth to insure Anne's daughter wasn't removed from Pemberley.

Still, she had some confidence in her promise. Elizabeth knew that Lady Catherine could take the baby regardless of what Elizabeth did, but, for now, it was clearly not safe for the baby to have a long journey on the road. She would fight if anyone endangered the baby.

Mrs. Darcy exhaled, her eyelids fluttering closed. Her hand slid from Elizabeth's arm and she froze, worried Mrs. Darcy was dead. Then, the frail form in the bed drew in a shuddering breath, and another, and Elizabeth backed away to sit in the chair. She stayed there, watching them both, until the baby work up. Wishing she dared wake Mrs. Darcy too, to say goodbye to her child, Elizabeth collected the baby. It didn't surprise her to learn that Mrs. Darcy died during the night.

Whether due to the sorrow that permeated the manor or her own frailty, the baby slipped into a decline upon her mother's death. Elizabeth got even less sleep than before, though she hadn't known that to be possible. The baby woke up frequently, but would only nurse for a few minutes. Elizabeth had to stay with her constantly, even when she fed, for sometimes it seemed as if Nelly didn't even bother waking up when she nursed.

After Mrs. Darcy's funeral, Elizabeth braced herself for an argument with Lady Catherine, but the Right Honorable Lady never appeared. Elizabeth assumed, since the baby was all that remained of Anne Darcy, that Lady Catherine would insist on taking her. She much was relieved to find that Mrs. Darcy's mother swept from Pemberley with as much presumption and as little love as she entered with.

A few hours after Lady Catherine left, Elizabeth was sitting in her room, holding the baby in her lap, when a maid announced, "Reverend Barton wants to see you. Shall I show him in?"

Elizabeth blinked blurrily at the maid. She realized she hadn't been aware of whether it was morning or night. "I'll go down. Will you stay with the baby until I return?" she asked.

The maid nodded.

Elizabeth handed her the infant. "If she wakes, take her to Nelly. Watch her while she nurses, and then bring her back to my room."

She briefly considered what she must look like, with her hair pinned up sloppily and wearing one of her oldest gowns, but decided she was decent. Moreover, she felt he should accept her state of disarray. If he wished a more formal meeting, he would have sent word ahead.

She was surprised when the maid directed her to the kitchen, but when she saw how muddy Reverend Barton was, she realized it made sense. He was sitting on a wooden stool. Someone brought a chair for Elizabeth. She realized that the sound of rain still filled her days and nights, a backdrop to the terrible world of frailty and death in which she was living.

He inquired after her health, but she could see that he was having difficulty keeping to the social niceties. "What brings you here, Reverend?"

"My duty. Lady Catherine insisted her daughter be buried in the Darcy cemetery. As it was a reasonable request, I acceded, although she has no authority in Pemberley. It's very odd, with Mr. Darcy's absence."

"Mrs. Reynolds wrote him after Mrs. Darcy died," Elizabeth said. "Mrs. Darcy forbade everyone to write him about her health."

"I understand that. With the rains, it's almost impossible to get through. I walked about six miles on a trail to get here."

"What is so urgent?" she asked.

"The baby hasn't been baptized. Normally, this wouldn't be a problem, but they say she isn't likely to live. Indeed, I understood from Lady Catherine that it is a miracle she's still alive."

"I can't authorize a baptism," Elizabeth protested, surprised he would suggest it. She was no relation to the family. "I don't know what name Mr. Darcy wants."

"You seem to be the only one who can. She was left in your care by her mother and grandmother." He paused, as if weighing his next words. "I know you aren't a member of my parish, Miss Bennet, but I feel it's my duty to point out the impropriety of you remaining in this house. If you wish to unburden yourself of decisions regarding this child, no one would criticize you. Rather, they may show you censure for staying."

Elizabeth hardly felt alone in a household with more servants

49

than she ever saw in one location, but she understood the point he was making. However respectable Mrs. Reynolds was, she was a housekeeper and not adequate to chaperone a young lady. But Elizabeth wouldn't leave the baby.

"No." She shook her head. "I can't leave her. Not while there's hope of her living."

"I understand," Reverend Barton said. She thought, even, that there was respect in his tone. "You obviously care deeply for the child. People are saying you're keeping her alive by sheer will. Don't let that care end at her corporal being. I leave the decision of the baptism to you."

Elizabeth nodded, resigned, asking to excuse herself for a moment. She once again sought out Mrs. Reynolds, but in this, the housekeeper was of little assistance. She declared she had no authority to even suggest a name for the baby, but agreed that baptism was important. Not very familiar with the female nomenclature of Anne Darcy's line, Elizabeth settled on Catherine Anne Darcy for the baby's name, feeling it showed respect in the proper places. She was still fretting about the suitability of her choice when the baptism took place.

After Reverend Barton left, Elizabeth looked down at the baby she held. Catherine seemed such an awfully big name for such a tiny baby. "Kate," Elizabeth whispered, trying the name out. Kate nuzzled the finger Elizabeth stroked along her cheek. She hoped that meant the baby was hungry. She took her upstairs, changing her out of the fine white gown her mother had sewn her. None of Kate's clothing fit her yet, all being too large, but Elizabeth wanted to set aside the dress she was christened in.

Chapter 8

By the following week, Kate was thriving. She would now sleep for nearly three hours at a time and nurse for ten or fifteen minutes. She still was smaller than Fitz was at birth, but she was gaining weight. Nevertheless, Elizabeth hadn't had three consecutive hours of sleep in a long time. If she wasn't bringing Kate to Nelly to be nursed, she was watching the nursing, since Nelly's tendency to fall asleep made Elizabeth afraid Nelly would roll on Kate. Elizabeth hardly noticed whether it was day or night. The sky was so gloomy and the rain was so constant that candles were needed at all times.

It was a rare moment of sound sleep for Elizabeth when someone startled her awake by opening the door to her room. If he knocked, she hadn't heard him. The darkness was nearly all encompassing, not telling her if it was late at night or very early in the morning, but a candle flame flickered as he strode purposefully toward the cradle. He leaned over Kate, holding the candle above her to illuminate her face. Angry that anyone should barge into her room and, worse, go near the baby, Elizabeth sat up, snapping, "Get out of my bedroom. Stay back from there. You have no right to be here!"

He turned toward her, the light of the candle now illuminating his face. To her shock and surprise, she recognized Mr. Darcy. He was covered in mud. "I'm sorry. I wanted to see my daughter."

Elizabeth slipped out of bed, mortified that she'd just reproached Mr. Darcy for wanting to see his child. Belatedly realizing she was only wearing a nightgown, she pulled a shawl over it and came to the cradle. "She should wake soon. She never sleeps very long." She hoped her tone conveyed her contrition for rebuking him.

"I apologize for intruding, and for not being here sooner. I didn't receive news about Anne until four days ago. Lady Catherine told me I had a daughter, but she wasn't likely to live long. She expected her to be dead before I arrived. I wasn't here for Anne. I wanted to be here for my daughter."

Numerous thoughts came to Elizabeth. How did Mr. Darcy

get to Pemberley, since the roads were impassible? Was the mail delayed that long? The roads must be worse than she thought. She wondered if the reassuring letters she wrote to her family ever arrived. But she voiced only one question. "Where did you see Lady Catherine?"

"She's staying at the Red Lion about ten miles south of here. The roads were too bad for her to continue. I walked from there." He looked down at himself and said, "I should clean up. I'm sorry for intruding," he repeated. He looked nearly as tired as she felt. He gave her a look she couldn't interpret, shook his head, and left.

Elizabeth still had no idea of the time, but she started readying for the day. While she was dressing, Kate woke up. She took her to Nelly and then downstairs into the parlor, asking a maid to light the fire, for them to sit beside.

Darcy came down, mud free, but with wet hair. Something about seeing him like that, tired and slightly disarrayed, sent a strange shiver through Elizabeth. It was, she realized, too intimate a state. No one should see Mr. Darcy like this but his wife. "Let me apologize again for my intrusion," he said a third time. "I wasn't thinking of anything but reaching my daughter before I lost her as well. I would like to hold her."

"Sit down first." She didn't mean for it to sound like an order, but she could see he was exhausted, and had the suspicion he had little practice holding infants. She didn't want him dropping Kate. She was exhausted too, and had spent too many of the past days giving orders she wasn't even in a position to give. Apparently unperturbed by her words or tone, Darcy sat. Elizabeth stood, crossing to hand Kate to him.

"Mr. Barton insisted on baptizing her. She is Catherine Anne Darcy. I'm sorry, but someone had to make a decision. I call her Kate."

"It's understandable," Darcy said. "I'm sorry I wasn't here. Why didn't you write me?"

"Write you? I can't write you a letter."

"It's what, three in the morning? You are alone with me here and you couldn't write me a letter?"

"I promised Mrs. Darcy."

"Sometimes promises need to be broken," he said. For the first time, his tone showed a discernable emotion, and it was anger.

"I got word to Lady Catherine. I made sure she knew you hadn't been informed. I assumed she would write you." Elizabeth didn't know why she was defending herself. She'd kept her word as

52

best she could, and done all she should. She was living, alone, in his giant empty manor taking care of his child. What right did he have to be angry with her?

"She didn't write me. She blames me and my daughter for Anne's death."

"That's a shoddy excuse," Elizabeth said. "Mrs. Darcy was alive when I wrote to her, and for quite some time after." She realized her words lacked tact, but she was much too tired to care. "I assume Mrs. Darcy wasn't forced to marry you. She was an adult and made the choice."

She was surprised at Darcy's bitter laugh. "No. She wasn't forced to marry me." He paused, as if contemplating saying something more, but only added, "She wanted to marry me and wanted a child."

Elizabeth noticed a footstool and moved it to where Mr. Darcy could use it. He put up his feet and continued to hold Kate. Elizabeth curled up in her chair and fell asleep. She awoke to Kate crying. Briefly, she wondered where she was. Her mind still foggy with sleep, she took in Darcy still holding Kate, rocking her in his arms and speaking softly to her. Elizabeth smiled.

"I suspect she's hungry," she said, coming fully awake. "Let me take her to the wet nurse."

"Wasn't she fed just before I came down?"

"Yes," Elizabeth replied. "But she gets hungry pretty quickly."

Darcy wanted his valet, his solicitor and someone to tell him how to deal with a tiny baby. He also wanted a chance to say goodbye to Anne. He couldn't be angry with Mrs. Reynolds, because he told her to obey Anne's orders. A part of him wanted to be angry with Elizabeth, but he knew that was unfair, too. She had no way of knowing the true extent of Lady Catherine's contrariness. Whatever else he could say about Mrs. Bennet, she cared for her children and wouldn't have hesitated to send him word under similar circumstances. Growing up with her, Elizabeth wouldn't be able to guess at the cold and vindictive nature of his aunt.

Besides, Mrs. Reynolds and the other servants not only informed him that Elizabeth had been a steadfast and caring companion for Anne, but also credited her with saving Kate's life. Everyone else, it seemed, gave up on her, a stance he was sure wasn't helped by Lady Catherine.

Darcy sighed, pacing the length of his study. He should send Elizabeth away, but with Nelly Douglas as wet nurse, he needed someone who would insist she nurse Kate as often as Kate needed to nurse. Kate was still too small, too frail, to be put into the care of someone who didn't love her. Seeing Elizabeth with her, hearing about how devotedly she tended Kate, Darcy knew Elizabeth was the one person, aside from himself, who truly loved his daughter. If he sent Elizabeth away, it might well cost him Kate.

If he kept Elizabeth, it might cost him his sanity. He'd already made the mistake of stopping again at Elizabeth's room to see his daughter. As it was early in the evening at the time, he hadn't expected her to already be prepared for bed. Her nightgown wasn't particularly thin, since it was still quite cold, but it was a nightgown. Sitting in his home with his daughter in her arms, she was the embodiment of all his dreams about her. When she looked up as he entered, love for Kate still shining in her eyes, it was all he could do not to fall on his knees and propose to her.

He could hardly court her. Not only was he in deep mourning, he dared not do anything to drive her away. His daughter's life appeared to depend on Elizabeth Bennet. It was all very well for people to say Kate was getting better, but he knew Nelly Douglas had to be awakened half the time she nursed Kate. During the day, she was fine. At night, she often slept through the lusty cries of her own son. She would certainly sleep through Kate's gentler cries. No, Elizabeth simply had to stay, as long as he could keep her.

After a week, he no longer considered Kate's cries gentle. He wasn't very near her, but somehow he heard her many times. Admittedly, he left his bedroom door open so that he could hear better. Kate woke up very often, much more often than he thought a baby should. Although he told himself he shouldn't, Darcy would creep down the hall, staying just out of sight, and listen. Elizabeth was always there, carrying Kate to the wet nurse, changing her, singing to her and holding her. He would lean against the wall and close his eyes, picturing Elizabeth and his daughter.

The rain finally stopped, and the sun made an attempt to dry up Pemberley. Relieved to be free of the exquisite torment of Elizabeth's presence, he rode out to inspect the damage, which was extensive. Three tenants' cottages were flooded and the road was impassible in several spots. Some stock was lost in the flooding. He put men to work on both domiciles and roads, glad that he could pay for as much labor as was needed. The initial inspection done and work groups deployed, Darcy urged his mount toward the manor. He found that as much as he'd longed to be free of the pain of being near Elizabeth, now he hurried home in hope of seeing her.

Lambton, his next inspection revealed, suffered worse, so he paid to have the roads rebuilt. The roads not on Pemberley property weren't his responsibility, but his father always maintained them and Darcy kept that tradition. He knew the whole region would suffer if the roads were impassible.

Mastering his fear it might make Elizabeth unnecessary, he sent for the wet nurse from Lambton to relieve Nelly Douglas, but found her child had died and she let her milk dry up. There were probably other possibilities, but he couldn't find time to look into them, the wet nurse for his child being a delicate choice. A voice in the back of his mind said that he was stalling because if he hired a competent wet nurse, Elizabeth would leave. He pretended he didn't hear that voice. He told himself he was leaving the situation as it was because he was terribly busy and Kate was thriving.

His rationalizing wasn't far from the truth, for Kate was growing stronger and the flooding had left much to do. In spite of the latter, he took to returning home early, for he found that Elizabeth dined and readied for bed in keeping with Kate's schedule, not staying up into the evening. If he wasn't home at a reasonable hour, he missed having dinner with her. He looked forward to their meals and wanted to prolong them, enjoying their talks filled with news of Kate and about the books Elizabeth read from his library, but often Kate needed her before they had a decent dinner.

Watching Elizabeth excuse herself and hurry away, interrupting yet another meal by responding to cries she was always the first to hear, he longed to hurry after her. To, just once, catch her up in his arms and hold her. He cherished his memory of her sitting in her room, holding Kate. He adored the way she laughed when he said something preposterous about a book, and found himself taking discussions of them down ridiculous paths, just to see her smile.

He sat down, realizing he'd risen when she left and never reseated himself. He couldn't court her, he knew. Her rejection, her words vivid in his mind, surly still held, no matter how she laughed at his foolishness or smiled at his daughter. Elizabeth made it clear then that she didn't love him, and he didn't dare do anything to drive her away now, such as pressing his suit. Kate was so tiny and so vulnerable. The clothing Anne made for her was too large, but they had nothing smaller.

Just that morning, he saw Kate in the same gown she wore when he first beheld her. Smiling, he realized it almost fit her now. He'd been home for almost a month, and Kate, if not thriving, was surely growing.

A month! Had it really been a month? There was so much

still to do. He would be able to work harder now. His valet had made it back to Pemberley. News had also arrived that Lady Catherine had safely reached Rosings. He hoped she would remember that, in truth, it was Kate's home. He fully expected his aunt to try to disinherit the granddaughter she'd declared both a murderess and dead.

Elizabeth wasn't exactly lying to her family when she wrote them that bad roads kept her at Pemberley, but she knew she wasn't telling the truth, either. When a plethora of letters finally arrived, they didn't include orders for her to return. Her letters never mentioned Mr. Darcy, but spoke often about Kate. She recognized she was compromised by living without a proper chaperone, but she considered Kate's health more important than her reputation. After all, if Lydia could survive her scandal, surely Elizabeth would be able to find someone to take her, eventually.

Not that she wanted anyone to take her, she realized. She was perfectly content as she was. Of course, this included walking the grounds of Pemberley, reading and discussing books from Mr. Darcy's library with Mr. Darcy, and caring for Kate. She knew this borrowed life she was living would have to come to an end eventually, but she resolved to do nothing to hasten it.

Which was why she held her tongue when confronted with Darcy's continued aloofness, although she was hurt by his formality. She enjoyed her conversations with him, and not only concerning books and Kate. She also found herself interested in the work he was doing to repair the damage of the flooding, both at Pemberley and in Lambton. She always suspected he was a good landlord, but his constant personal attention to this impressed her. He obviously no longer loved her, because he was always very correct and formal with her, but she flattered herself that he at least did not find her presence displeasing.

Their days fell into such an easy routine that she was taken aback one day when a maid requested her presence in the parlor. That she just put Kate down, something Mr. Darcy would know, only added to her unease. Why would he send for her after seeing her so recently, and when he knew she was without any legitimate means of refusal?

Elizabeth was so perturbed by this uncharacteristic summons that she was forced to acknowledge the mounting tension in herself. She knew she was living without assurance of her place, but Darcy's summons spurred a disquiet in her that bordered on fear, and she did not like that at all. A small part of her hoped he was about to cast her out. At least she could return to her family and a life where she knew her role was sure. Even thinking this as she marched toward the parlor, she resolved to fight. She would not leave Kate.

Mr. Darcy, seeming more aloof than was his custom of late, greeted her at the door of the parlor. He practically hovered as he walked her to a chair, expressing a nervousness she was unaccustomed to associating with him. It served to increase her own worry tenfold.

"Miss Bennet," Mr. Darcy began after she was seated. He didn't sit, but rather stood before her. "Reverend Barton called my attention to something that cannot be ignored any longer. I am very grateful for your care of my daughter, but in providing it, you have ruined your reputation irretrievably. You know I would be happy to marry you, but I explained to Mr. Barton that you do not reciprocate these feelings. Nevertheless, he thinks it necessary for us to marry. I agree. With your permission, I would like to allow him to post the banns."

Elizabeth stared at him, then shut her mouth, realizing she left it gaping open. Was he proposing to her again? And what did he just say, that he would be happy to marry her? Happy wasn't the word she wanted to associate with marriage. The marriage she wanted required love, joy, passion and devotion. "You don't need to do this," she said. "I had to stay for Kate."

"If you don't marry me, you will have to leave Kate eventually. You are acting the part of a nursemaid. I could hire you to that position, but you are the daughter of a gentleman and it's unsuitable. You really don't have an alternative."

At least she understood his tension now. If his previous proposal was insulting, this one was equally so. He was offering to marry her because Kate needed her and because she was accidentally compromised. It would make him happy to have his daughter well cared for. Of course it would, and he would get a presumably biddable and, he probably thought, eternally grateful, wife. A bride who would be forever in his debt for not kicking her to the street, sullied and prospectless.

Elizabeth looked down, taking a deep breath to rein in her anger. She had to set her resentment toward Darcy aside and deliberate on what was most important. Kate needed her and, she admitted, she needed Kate. She couldn't leave her. Elizabeth always expected to love her own children and suspected she would love her nieces and nephews. She never expected to love a child totally unrelated to her. Especially not enough to overcome her unwillingness to marry Mr. Darcy in the face of his continued insults.

Yet, her love for Kate did.

Her emotions under control, she looked up at him. Darcy loomed over her chair, strain apparent in every muscle. Her hand twitched of its own volition, and she had to restrain herself from reaching out to sooth him. She searched his eyes, seeing only worry, her mind roaming through memories of every pleasant meal spent talking. To her surprise, she had a ready inventory of his smile, of their hands accidentally clasping when they reached for the same book, of him holding Kate in his arms, gazing at her with a father's love.

Was she really that unwilling to marry him? He showed no signs of his past attraction to her, but she realized her attitude toward him had changed. She respected him. She enjoyed his company. Where once he seemed aloof, now he seemed simply restrained, and it gave her pleasure to draw him out.

She looked down again, confused. No, she couldn't love Darcy. He didn't love her. She refused to dote on a man whom she made merely happy. Her pride wouldn't allow it. Any attraction she felt must be because he was the only person of her class she'd seen for the last month. It was only proximity to him that spurred these fanciful notions. It could be nothing more than that.

"Very well," she said, realizing she was tormenting him with her silence. "I am twenty-one and could marry without it, but I would like to obtain my father's permission."

"Of course, but Kate can't travel yet, so we can't go to Longbourn. I propose we marry here. We can have a quiet ceremony."

Was he ashamed of her, then? Elizabeth stiffened. Perhaps she'd agreed too quickly, but she wouldn't go back on her word. "No. I want my family with me, at least Jane and my father."

"Invite whomever you like," he said, sounding frustrated. He turned away, his hands clenched at his sides. "I have family I want as well. Georgiana is betrothed, but she should be here. Under the circumstances, do not invite Mr. Wickham, even if he is your brother now."

"Very well," Elizabeth said. She'd had no intension of doing so. She didn't care for Wickham and would never be that insensitive to Darcy, but the way he said it, making it an order, offended her. Her earlier fear was already realized. He expected a docile, grateful wife. "If I am excused, then," she said, making it a statement, not a question. He nodded, not turning around, and Elizabeth all but stormed from the room.

Darcy realized with Elizabeth's parents, three sisters, and the Gardiners attending the wedding, his side would look very thin unless he invited someone. He didn't want it to appear to Elizabeth that he was ashamed of the marriage. He replayed their exchange in the parlor many times, aware that he had offended her somehow, and settled on his suggestion of a quiet ceremony as the moment things went truly wrong. A moment before that, the way she looked at him, he almost thought she cared for him.

He suggested a quiet ceremony because he thought she would want one, but now realized he made a mistake. One he seemed doomed to keep making. Instead of asking Elizabeth for her thoughts, he decided what they must be and acted on them. Must he always be so great a buffoon with her? Perhaps, he thought ruefully, he was that way with everyone. No one else stood up to him the way Elizabeth did.

To try to mitigate the damage, he wrote an announcement of his wedding and sent invitations to a fairly large number of relatives and friends, promising them housing in Pemberley. None of the missives were particularly detailed, for he felt he needed to explain the true circumstances of the marriage in person. He didn't want anything misconstrued, or for letters to exist where he wrote about Elizabeth's reputation being compromised.

He invited Colonel Fitzwilliam to stand with him at the ceremony, and invited Bingley and his sisters to attend. It didn't surprise him that Bingley's sisters declined. Bingley himself wrote that he was pleased to come. The letter was brief and correct, but Darcy could almost feel the surprise and, he imagined, recrimination, that went into ever pen stroke. Knowing as he now did, that Jane Bennet had truly loved his friend, and seeing the continued constancy of Bingley's feelings for Elizabeth's sister, Darcy was willing to assume guilt for his role in deterring their union. Perhaps he would find a way to make amends for that, as well. It seemed, he mused, that he had much to atone for.

The need for a quick wedding resulted in the one person whose presence he really cared about being absent, Georgiana. Her wedding date was already set, and would take place less than a week before his wedding to Elizabeth. He considered pushing his wedding back, but Kate was doing so well, and Elizabeth seemed so distant, he feared she might change her mind and leave.

To further add to the turmoil in his life, he received a letter from the uncle of Georgiana's fiancé which was tantamount to an urgent summons to London. It appeared Georgiana, always the sweet and trusting soul, confided to her husband-to-be, Viscount Lawrence, everything that happened between her and Wickham. The viscount brought it up with the uncle who raised him, and the uncle promptly attempted to blackmail Darcy into increasing Georgiana's dowry.

Darcy was torn. He knew Elizabeth was perfectly capable of arranging for the ceremony and caring for the arriving guests. Of her proficiencies, he had no concerns, but these were his final moments alone with her before the wedding. He'd hoped to apologize for his, second, inept proposal. If he could catch a glimmer, just a spark, of what he once imagined he saw in her eyes when she looked at him, he would tell her all. He would admit that Anne lay in wait for him, playing on his dejection. He would confess that his love for Elizabeth never wavered, in all these months. Surely, such ardor would fan a spark into a flame.

Yet Georgiana needed him, and depended on him, so he hurried off to London. Darcy would, he reasoned, have years to make amends with Elizabeth and win her over. His sister needed him now. Besides, if the matter were handled quickly enough, there would still be time to speak to Elizabeth. Darcy harbored hopes of marrying a woman who loved him, and this was his last chance.

It took delicate negotiations on Darcy's part to persuade the Lawrences to keep quiet about Georgiana's secret without giving them money. Not that he couldn't afford it, but Darcy resented blackmail on principle. For good measure, he made certain he had a letter from the young Viscount's uncle that indicated he knew about the intended elopement. If the uncle ever brought the information to public attention, that letter would say that he knew about the situation, as did other members of the family, but encouraged the wedding to proceed. To Darcy's vast relief, Georgiana's husband stood at his side and argued against extortion.

By the time the incident was put to rest, an exasperated Darcy realized there was no point in returning to Pemberley before Georgiana's wedding. He would only have to turn around and go back to London. Manfully suppressing his troubles, he acted the proper guardian, for the last few days Georgiana was in his care. When her wedding day came, Darcy found himself both proud and, though he didn't let it show, oddly melancholy.

Watching his sister and her new husband look at each other with love in their eyes, Darcy realized he was losing one dream and desperately worried for another. Though he was happy for Georgiana, and overjoyed that her new husband so clearly adored her, he was saddened that she would never live with him and Elizabeth.

It seemed long ago now, but he held dreams of them becoming quite close and of watching his timid sister bloom under Elizabeth's example. It was, he knew, the same thing he hoped for Kate. Seeing Georgiana now the possession of another man stirred fatherly feelings in him, giving him a glimpse of how it would be, someday, when Kate wed.

The other dream, though in some ways more attainable, seemed almost as hopeless. Yet Darcy vowed, watching his sister and her new husband, that he would not give up on it. Whatever it took, someday Elizabeth would look at him like that, with love in her eyes. Not just the lingering joy that wreathed her features when she looked up from Kate, captivating though he found it, but true love, for him. First, he had to make sure he didn't say or do anything else to upset her, for Elizabeth was strong willed and wouldn't go through with the wedding if too provoked. Then, once she was his, he would have the rest of their lives to gain her love.

Chapter 9

Though she was angry with him, Elizabeth was still hurt that Darcy chose to spend most of the time between the engagement and the wedding away from her. If she had any lingering notion that he still loved her, his behavior seemed designed to lay it to rest. Of course, she told herself, she knew he didn't love her, for she saw him with the first Mrs. Darcy. Yet, it wasn't just a lack of love, or his grief for his lost wife. He kept a formality between them that was greater than it ever was before, seemingly designed to deliberately hurt her.

She began to nourish a secret fear that he blamed her for not writing him about Anne Darcy, even though she thought Lady Catherine would and even though there was nothing he could have done to save his wife. Yes, he'd been cordial, even kind, but that was before the proposal. Maybe he wished he hadn't asked. The hypocrisy of marrying the woman he blamed for his first wife's death might outweigh his love for his daughter.

Elizabeth harbored these fears and fancies as her family and friends gathered. She told herself they were foolish, but Darcy's behavior seemed to confirm them. His continued absence, accompanied by letters telling vaguely of business that he must attend to, was obviously designed to remove himself from her presence. Not only did it seem he couldn't bear to be around her as their wedding day approached, it was embarrassing for Darcy not to be there, making it difficult for her to enjoy seeing her family.

When Darcy finally returned, she found him equally remote with her family. She knew he had a long talk with her father, but that did nothing to make the two men get along. Mr. Bennet spent his time in Darcy's library. Mrs. Bennet was awed by Pemberley at first, but soon was making suggestions to Elizabeth on how it could be run better. Her family still didn't understand her need to see to Kate, who was gaining weight and thriving. The told her that if the wet nurse was inadequate, another should be found, now that the roads were passable. Elizabeth couldn't make them understand that she feared to change what was working. As her anxieties grew, the only person she could even bare to be around was Jane.

The day before the ceremony was to take place, she and Jane were walking the grounds together, removing themselves from their mother and sisters. Jane, Elizabeth knew, was also eager to stay away because Mr. Bingley was to arrive that afternoon. That she didn't wish to see him could be read on her face, but Elizabeth was uncertain of the root of the emotion. Was her sister still in love with Mr. Bingley and the sight of him too painful, or did sweet and biddable Jane harbor anger in her breast? She was considering asking, as a much more interesting topic than silently mulling over her own troubles, when Jane spoke.

"Look, Elizabeth, your future husband," she said, her tone warm.

Elizabeth glanced in the direction her sister pointed. She hadn't realized they were so near the edge of the trees, but a gap in the foliage revealed Mr. Darcy riding across an open meadow. She had mixed feelings about him riding the day before her wedding. On one hand, she knew he was personally inspecting the road repair, which was vital to the community. On the other hand, she resented he wasn't spending time with her and her family. The fact that his reason for avoiding everyone was valid did little to mitigate his appearing to be a neglectful host.

As a child, Elizabeth sometimes imagined her wedding day. The face of the groom was always hazy, but the figure of Mr. Darcy more than lived up to her youthful fantasies. He was tall and moved with a grace that showed he spent a great deal of time on outdoor activities. He was lean, muscular, and his face was handsome, more handsome than any other man she knew. She once thought her father was the most handsome man she knew, but now she had a higher standard.

"You do love him," Jane said.

Elizabeth turned to see her sister was looking at her, not the well-cut figure of her fiancé. "I don't know," she said, looking away from Jane's gaze.

"I do, and I'm glad," Jane said. Smiling, she took Elizabeth's arm, turning her back toward Pemberley.

Darcy was terribly nervous on his wedding day, as he waited for Elizabeth to appear. He hadn't felt any such jitters when he wed Anne. In fact, he thought, he hadn't felt much of anything. Now, he was inexplicable worried as he waited beside the altar, fearing that anything should yet again come between him marrying Elizabeth.

His first glimpse of her took his breath away. He was used to seeing her tired from staying up with Kate, slightly frazzled and in

63

adorable disarray. Now, she looked stunningly beautiful, even more so than the first time he saw her. Today, resplendent in her gown, she was perfection.

No, that wasn't true. She needed, rather, deserved, rich jewelry, not the simple cross on a chain. A slight smile came to his lips. He would see she had jewelry worthy of her beauty. He would spend the rest of his life giving her everything she deserved. Watching her approach, he felt himself relax. What seemed at times so impossible a dream, was finally about to come true.

Elizabeth looked up as she neared the altar, meeting his gaze. He thought, he hoped, that there was a glimmer of affection in her eyes. He felt his facade of indifference wavering. He didn't need to hide his love any longer. He couldn't chase her away now. She was steps from his side.

The door to the church burst open, and a voice called out, "Stop the ceremony!" All eyes turned. It was his aunt, Lady Catherine. Darcy took a step back, half in surprise at her words and half in shock at having his dream-turned-reality shattered.

"Stop the ceremony!" Lady Catherine repeated forcefully. "It cannot go on."

"Why ever not?" Mrs. Bennet asked, standing.

"His wife is barely cold in her grave. He can't marry that seductress."

"His wife is gone," Mrs. Bennet said. "And my daughter is no seductress! How dare you malign her on her wedding day!"

Elizabeth had only half turned, so Darcy could see the color drain from her face. She took a step backward, toward him.

"Darcy loved Anne," Lady Catherine said, marching up the aisle. "He would never dishonor her memory by marrying so soon, and so far beneath him, unless seduced. I am here to save him."

A few strides brought Darcy to Elizabeth's side before his aunt could reach her. Without thinking, he put his arm protectively around her. She leaned into him, quenching his quick fear that she might pull away. He was aware of Bingley and Jane leaving their posts as well, taking up position on either side of him and Elizabeth, and Fitzwilliam moving to stand behind them. Under his arm, Elizabeth trembled.

Lady Catherine came to a stop before them, her wrinkled face suffused with anger. She glared up at Darcy and Elizabeth, then around the church. "You all know she's been living in his house, alone. Placing herself forever in his sight. Endlessly beguiling him with her dewy country airs."

Beside him, Elizabeth sputtered, and Darcy realized she shook with anger, not fear. Darcy could sympathize. He was having trouble gathering himself to speak as well, too astonished by his aunts ridiculous accusations.

Mrs. Bennet looked around the church, her face red with anger. "Who is this ghastly woman?" she demanded.

"Who am I?" Lady Catherin's voice went up nearly an octave. "I am Lady Catherine de Bourgh and Darcy is my son!"

"If he were your son, he would be Mr. de Bourgh," Mr. Bennet said quietly, rising from his seat next to Mrs. Bennet.

"He married my daughter, you fool. He is my son, and I say this marriage cannot take place."

"Aunt Catherine," Darcy said, finally finding his voice. He tried to take a soothing tone. "Be reasonable."

"I am reasonable. You are marrying into a family that is not only beneath you, but will put a stain on both of our houses." She took a step closer, all but yelling into his face. "Why, one daughter's marriage was a patched up affair, at your expense. The oldest girl can't even keep a suitor. She was expected to marry someone and he left her dangling. He probably got what he wanted and left her."

Beside him, Bingley jerked as if struck. "Is that what they're saying about Miss Bennet?" he demanded. "How can they insult her so? She's the loveliest, kindest, sweetest, woman there is. I would ask her to marry me in a heartbeat, if I thought she loved me."

"You would?" Jane asked, a blush appeared on her lovely face. She stepped around Elizabeth to see him better, apparently unaware she was moving between Lady Catherine and Darcy. "I do lo—"

"No," Bingley interrupted her. "It's unfair to make you say it in so public a place. Not without a proper proposal." He joined her before Darcy and Elizabeth, sinking to one knee. "I love you and have loved you since I first met you. I was persuaded you didn't love me. I never meant to hurt you. If they are saying that about you, I owe you a proposal, and if you say yes, you would take this weight off my heart that has been there ever since I left you. I don't want to force you into a marriage you don't wish for, but if it eases you even a little, please accept me. I won't be happy unless you marry me."

Miss Bennet held out both of her hands. "I love you," she said as he took her hands. "I never wanted to say it or even let people guess it, but I love you. I'll tell everyone here, I'll tell the world. There was no weight on your heart. It was the bond that drew it to mine."

If Darcy saw half the love in Elizabeth's face as he saw in Miss Bennet's, he would be happy. He wasn't surprised when

Bingley stood, took Jane in his arms, and kissed her. He was happy for his friend, even in view of such an unorthodox proposal. Looking around, it appeared as if most people in the congregation were equally happy.

But not all of them. "This is the family you are marrying into? Men proposing to women in the middle of a sacred ceremony? This unseemly display is unworthy of your heritage," Lady Catherine said, glaring at Bingley and Miss Bennet as they rose and stepped away from her anger.

"My heritage is in the hands of the baby in the back of the church and the woman next to me, who will raise that baby," Darcy said, unable and unwilling to restrain the anger in his tone, too badgered by his aunt's hubris and hypocrisy. "And you best keep that firmly in mind, because Kate will inherit Rosings."

"That baby is not Anne's daughter. My granddaughter was too frail to survive. You hope to foist on me some peasant's child and pretend it has a claim to Rosings? And what kind of name is Kate? It has no dignity."

"Her name is Catherine," Elizabeth said, her tone sharp and cold as ice. "And I will prove to you she's your daughter's daughter." Pulling away from Darcy, Elizabeth walked over to Nelly and uncovered Kate's six-toed foot. "Anne's feet were like this."

"How dare you disclose Anne's deformity! You are unworthy of the name Darcy. You have no right to even be here. The only way you can get a husband is the same way your sisters did: by improper behavior."

"Miss Bennet never did anything improper," Bingley said, ironically holding his betrothed much too close. Far from objecting to the impropriety of their embrace, Jane gazed up at Bingley with adoration, seemingly unaware Lady Catherine even spoke of them.

"Neither did Lydia," Mrs. Bennet said, though Darcy doubted that was true. "You may be a lady, but you aren't acting like one. You come to a wedding where you weren't even invited and make false accusations and try to claim other people are wrong. Get out. The wedding will go on."

"You impertinent—"

"Get out! Leave. My daughters behave much better than you do."

Darcy was afraid Mrs. Bennet and his aunt would come to blows. "Leave," he said in a deliberately quiet voice, hoping Lady Catherine would regain her calm if presented with his. "This wedding will take place. Kate needs a mother." And I need a wife, he

66

thought. A wife whom I love.

"I will not be chased out by this low person," Lady Catherine said, indicating Mrs. Bennet.

"Then someone will take you out bodily," Mrs. Bennet said smugly. "And I will be the only grandmother Kate will ever know."

Shocked, Lady Catherine turned back to Darcy. Though he was trying to exercise restraint, Darcy knew his face must reveal both anger and disgust at his aunt's behavior. Taking a long look at him, she sat down and muttered, "Anne did say I had to be nice to her." Darcy had no idea of what she was talking about. Much louder, Lady Catherine proclaimed, "You may proceed, since you won't see reason. And her name is Catherine, not Kate."

Chapter 10

The guests left, some right after the wedding breakfast and others later in the afternoon. Darcy was relieved he and Elizabeth would have Pemberley to themselves, though there was already talk of a celebration for Bingley's and Jane's engagement. They dined blissfully alone and, for once, Kate didn't interrupt dinner, yet conversation didn't flourish. He apologized for his aunt's behavior and Elizabeth apologized for her mother's, but they didn't really discuss anything important.

Elizabeth seemed somehow remote. More so than any time since his poorly worded second proposal and definitely more than a new bride should. Darcy was torn between professing his love, which he hoped would thaw her demeanor, and fear of saying anything to make matters more strained between them.

Worse than that, his mind whispered, what if he confessed his love and she remained unswayed? He'd never been so fearful of rejection before. Why had he set his heart on the one woman in England who appeared not to dote on him?

After a meal spent trying to read Elizabeth's silences, Darcy approached the bed chamber with as much trepidation as anticipation. He hadn't felt so unsure since boyhood. More than anything, he longed to make Elizabeth happy on their wedding night.

He entered the room and crossed to the bed, unable to take his eyes from her, even had he wanted to. She was sitting against the headboard, her hair loose about her. He'd seen it in braids, he'd seen it up. Now, he wanted to see it caressing her breasts. Even if she didn't love him as he wished, yet, he knew there was fire in Elizabeth. Surely, he could ignite passion between them.

He reached for her, longing to remove the delicate nightgown that stood between him and paradise.

Then he heard a wail from down the hall.

Elizabeth automatically jumped when she heard Kate cry. She

knew Kate's hunger was no longer life-threatening, but the cries tore her eyes from her new husband toward the bedroom door. She glanced back at Darcy, questioning. Where moments ago she dared to think she saw passion, there was now something darkly unreadable in his gaze. He stepped back, gesturing for her to go.

It pained her when he did so. She knew, as he said it often enough, that he only married her for Kate, but she'd hoped this one night, at least, they would be as lovers. It was, after all, their wedding night.

Letting her loose hair fall around her face to hide both anger and hurt, Elizabeth hurried from the room. She took Kate to Nelly and watched her nurse. Kate didn't fall asleep after she was finished, but fussed. Elizabeth picked her up and walked her back and forth, knowing that to put her down fussy would only lead to more crying. It was over an hour before Kate finally slept soundly enough for Elizabeth to put her in her crib, but she still fretted in her sleep, leaving Elizabeth tense with worry.

She returned to her bedroom to find Darcy sitting in a chair, reading. Reading? How could he read on their wedding night? "She's asleep, but will probably wake up soon. I think she has colic." Elizabeth said.

"I'm glad you're so good a mother to her," Darcy said, looking up from the page. He placed a finger to make his spot, the act fanning Elizabeth's anger.

"Isn't that why you married me?" she snapped. "Because you love Kate?"

"Of course, but I also proposed to you out of love."

"Which time?" she said, aware her tone was sullen.

Her heart leapt at his words, but to her mind they sounded like platitudes. Once, just once, she wished he would show passion toward her. Not cold reason, or logic, or well-rehearsed phrases. Ever since his second proposal, she was beginning to wonder if she'd imagined the closeness and rare smiles that lead her to accept. She certainly hadn't seen them since. Could they have been Darcy's attempt at seduction, and she actually fell into it? That he hadn't needed to muster more than the occasional smile to beguile her into this marriage stung her.

He slammed the book shut, standing. "Certainly you must know I proposed out of love the first time," he said. "I proposed out of love when there was absolutely no advantage to marrying you."

Elizabeth glared up at him, his words no longer affecting even her heart. So, he readily confessed that he proposed out of love only the first time, but not the second. He only proposed again because he compromised her and because she saved Kate. She pointed toward the door. She didn't need love from a man made almost entirely of stone. Kate's love would be enough. "I think you should leave," she said angrily.

After glaring at her for a moment, he tossed the book into the chair and left.

Elizabeth stood where she was, listening to his steps moving away. They paused, and she was filled with the irrational hope that he was coming back, but then they continued. Once she could no longer hear him, she crawled back into bed. Realizing she obviously married a man who was still in love with his dead wife, Elizabeth wrapped her arms around herself, squeezing into tight ball, and cried.

Kate woke three more times that night, though Elizabeth was only asleep the third time, having spent half the night in tears herself. Each time Kate woke, she cried unless Elizabeth walked her, even after being fed. When Kate's cries filled the house a fourth time it was morning. A maid brought breakfast into Nelly's room, where Elizabeth watched Kate nurse. "Mr. Darcy's orders," the maid said.

He always treats his servants well, Elizabeth thought bitterly. He wouldn't want his nursemaid to suffer from hunger. Kate still needed attention, but Elizabeth desperately needed sleep. She asked the maid to stay and watch Kate finish nursing, and stumbled to her bed. Elizabeth didn't know for how long she was asleep when Darcy came into her room and woke her.

He was saying something she didn't understand, but finally the fog lifted and she heard, "Georgiana needs me. I have to go." He left.

When the door closed, Elizabeth found herself wide awake. She took her pillow and threw it at the door. Not only did they not have a wedding night, she couldn't keep her husband interested in her for a single day. He hadn't even kissed her goodbye.

For the next several days, Kate occupied her time as much as she had when she was newborn. She developed a fever, which alarmed Elizabeth. Four days after the wedding, Kate slept for nearly the entire day, and alarm turned to fear.

Angry with him or no, Elizabeth was worried she would have to write to Darcy soon. Perhaps he could bring a physician from London and, if Kate didn't get better, he would want to be there. His words the night he barged into her bedchamber came back to her. He would want to say goodbye to his daughter. The very thought pressed Elizabeth into tears. She resolved to wait one more day, unwilling to accept what writing him would mean.

Then, that evening, she picked Kate up after a late feeding to find her skin less hot and no longer sweaty. Gratefully, Elizabeth realized the fever had broken. She smiled down at Kate, filled with relief, and Kate smiled back. It was the first time Kate had ever smiled, and the sight of it filled Elizabeth with joy, taking away days of sorrow, fear and anger.

"She smiled," she told Nelly, aware that she all but grinning as she said it.

"Most of them smile younger," Nelly said, to Elizabeth's chagrin. Nelly must have sensed Elizabeth's displeasure, because she continued. "But she was born too early and that puts them back. She's smiling now, which is all that matters."

Although Elizabeth was delighted with Kate's smiles, she wasn't happy that Kate's illness led her to decide that nighttime was a good time to be awake and daytime was for sleeping. After several days of this, Elizabeth started waking Kate during the day. She didn't like to make Kate cry, but was overjoyed that Kate was strong enough to be put on a more normal schedule of sleep.

With Kate out of danger from what everyone assured her was a minor illness and sleeping better at night now than ever before, Elizabeth had leisure to brood over Darcy's continued absence. Kate's smiles encouraged her, but they weren't enough. She was worried about their marriage and feeling she was becoming her mother. She felt very ill used. She received a brief note from Darcy saying Georgiana was better and he would not be home for at least a month.

Well, she would spend that month making a few changes. She didn't want to erase the existence of Anne, but she was now mistress of Pemberley and she had some authority. She would start in her bedroom.

After making a few minor changes while fuming about Darcy, she calmed enough to realize he must have told her what Georgiana was recovering from while she was still asleep. After thinking it through, she swallowed her pride and wrote a letter asking him what happened. She was pleased to get an answer almost as quickly as one could arrive. Darcy wrote that the day after Georgiana's wedding, she and her husband were in a carriage accident. Her husband was killed and Georgiana was injured.

Elizabeth was horrified. All this time, she was blaming Darcy for leaving her. Of course he should have gone to help Georgiana. The rest of the letter concerned Georgiana's family, who wanted

Georgiana to stay until they were certain whether or not she was pregnant.

Elizabeth wrote Darcy a letter thanking him for the explanation and detailing Kate's progress. She wrote Georgiana a cheerful letter with little real content. Georgiana's return letter was dictated to Darcy, because her arm was broken. Her left arm was fine, but she couldn't write with it. That gave Elizabeth an idea. She found the name of Georgiana's music master and wrote him a request.

Darcy was beginning to think that perhaps he and his sister were under a curse. First, Georgiana almost eloped with Wickham. Then, Anne all but tricked him into marrying her. Both his and Georgiana's recent weddings nearly failed to take place. Now, Georgiana's husband was dead and Georgiana had a broken arm and cracked ribs. It made him despair of ever having a chance to win Elizabeth's love.

Georgiana's deceased husband's relatives tried to get her to renounce her claims against the estate, even giving up her dowry. Darcy sent for his doctor from London for Georgiana's health and two lawyers for her financial wellbeing. When Darcy decided she was well enough to travel, they returned to Pemberley. Georgiana was now a widow with more money than she had before she was married and would be addressed as Lady Lawrence. She was also a sixteen year old girl who lost her husband. Her husband's family was no support and she was a more tempting target for fortune hunters than ever before.

Darcy needed Elizabeth to care for Georgiana as well as Kate. He wanted her as a wife, but he needed her for those he was responsible for. He couldn't offend her. While Georgiana was getting settled, Darcy knocked on the door of the room connecting to his bedroom, the one Anne had occupied and Elizabeth slept in on their wedding night. Upon entering, he was pleased to see the ghastly furniture Anne brought from Rosings had been removed. A few pieces from other rooms were in their place. There were also different pictures on the walls and the green curtains were replaced with brown ones. The most noticeable change was that a crib for Kate was in a corner of the room. That sent a message to Darcy: he wasn't welcome.

"I wanted to talk to you about Georgiana," he said to Elizabeth. He knew he'd already said something wrong, because Elizabeth seemed to freeze. But this was too important for him to be

72

silent on. "Anne chided me for not giving full information about her. If you read my letter, you know about her past with Wickham."

"I read it."

"You should know how her husband's family treated her. They tried to get her to sign away her widow's rights before her arm was set. They behaved terribly toward her. She is grieving for her husband and wondering why his family hated her so. You should know about it if you deal with her."

"You expect me to deal with her?" she asked.

Why was she so angry? "I was hoping you could. You're so good with Kate."

"I'll try," she said.

Darcy retreated to his bedroom to prepare for dinner. He wasn't very hopeful of Elizabeth accomplishing anything. She hadn't seemed to take to the idea at all. He was a bit surprised, for the one time they were together, Elizabeth and his sister seemed to get along well.

It wasn't until the next day that he realized Elizabeth had already planned to help Georgiana. He heard music. Surely, there were too many notes being played for one pair of hands. Georgiana couldn't play. He followed the sounds and saw Georgiana and Elizabeth playing the pianoforte. Georgiana played only with her left hand and Elizabeth played with both hands.

Over the next several days, Elizabeth seemed to reach Georgiana through music. Kate helped too, smiling at Georgiana. Elizabeth even managed to persuade her that she looked beautiful in black. Soon, it seemed there was a crowd of women in his life, all of whom he loved and all of whom were almost ignoring him. Georgiana lost her shyness with Elizabeth, and Kate smiled at Elizabeth and Georgiana more than she smiled at Darcy, who felt awkward with her.

Still, he was fairly content, if a bit confused and uncertain how to proceed. He'd never needed to win a woman before, as they always threw themselves at him. Even if it was an area where he was skilled, how did one court one's own wife, especially with a widowed younger sister and a daughter underfoot?

Chapter 11

Elizabeth knew she appeared happy. In fact, she was happy, for the most part. Darcy was no longer at all cold to her. She thought he may even be warming to her. She couldn't get herself to play the seductress, however, too afraid of rejection and with visions of his care toward Anne and Lady Catherine's accusations swimming through her head. She also discarded thoughts of confronting him. What good would it do to demand he love her and visit her bedchamber? It was be as shaming as shameful.

Their days soon settled into an agreeable routine, further increasing Elizabeth's reluctance toward confrontation. Things were so pleasant, she didn't want to risk change. Everything was correct, and nice. She and Darcy spoke of books again. She and Georgiana played the piano with both hands after her arm healed. Kate grew and started grabbing everything and putting it in her mouth. Elizabeth's life was very content, if a bit lacking. She knew many married couples rarely engaged in relations. She told herself what she and Darcy had wasn't much different than that.

As Kate grew, Elizabeth was pleased to unpack more of the clothing Anne sewed for her. She enjoyed sorting through the delicate garments, taking in the love and care Anne put into ever stitch. When Kate actually outgrew some of the clothing, Elizabeth set it aside carefully, not to be passed on, so that Kate would have this gift from her mother.

Unlike most of her activities, Elizabeth selected new items from Anne's carefully stowed work alone. It was a responsibility she cherished. It made her feel closer to the woman who was Kate's true mother, who Elizabeth had the honor of calling friend. One evening, after dinner and after Georgiana went to bed and Darcy retired to the library, Elizabeth took herself off to the solace of that task, communing, in a way, with the one woman who might understand the life she was living.

Sorting through the gowns, she removed a carefully wrapped bundle. Opening it revealed a garment oddly out of form with the others. Far from showing Anne's usual level of refinement or the gender nonspecificity of her other work, this dress was completely embroidered in flowers. Around and around, starting with small flowers about the neckline and growing to palm sized ones about the hem.

Elizabeth stared at it, wondering what could have possessed Anne to make such a thing. It reminded her of nothing so much as the garish furnishings Anne brought with her from Rosings, which had been kept, though they were ugly, to one day be given to Kate as some evidence of her mother's existence. Elizabeth traced Anne's work, still exceptional in spite of the lack of taste displayed. Around and around went overly bright lilies, irises and daffodils.

She blinked, holding the dress out at arm's length. Lily, iris, daffodil. Lid! It was just like the desk from Rosings! It was a message, a message only Elizabeth would understand. Anne sent her a message.

Where had they put that desk? Somewhere on the third floor. Elizabeth set the garment aside, jumping up, certain it there was meaning behind Anne's embroidery. Systematically, she searched the third floor rooms until she found the desk. Hands shaking slightly, unsure if she was being foolish or cleaver, she moved the three flowers Anne had shown her. Lifting the lid of the compartment, she found a letter.

Elizabeth stared at the sealed envelope. Miss Elizabeth Bennet was inscribed on it in Anne's hand. Elizabeth felt a wave of unease, confronted with such strong evidence that Anne's will was still at work in Pemberley. Unlike Kate's garments, which comforted her, holding a letter from Darcy's dead first wife made Elizabeth feel like she was living another woman's life. A stolen life.

Should she take the letter to Darcy? After all, she was not Miss Elizabeth Bennet any longer, and Anne was his wife. Shouldn't he have the decision of what to do with her property? Yet, the dress was obviously left for Elizabeth to find, and it was clearly addressed to her, even if her name had changed in a way Anne could never have foreseen.

Shaking her head at thoughts of reading the letter with him watching, or allowing him to read it first, Elizabeth retreated to her favorite reading nook, lighting candles about her. She was glad Georgiana had already retired and that Darcy was still ensconced in his library. No one else would presume to ask whose letter she read.

With a slightly trembling hand, Elizabeth broke the seal on the envelope. She removed the carefully folded pages and opening them.

My Dear Miss Bennet,

Please find it in yourself not to dislike me for what I am about to tell. I must lead with that, for you are a generous hearted creature and will not refuse my plea. There are certain truths I feel I must impart to you, though they may not place me in the most favorable of light. Take this as both my apology and amends. For my part, I had no wish to harm you. At first, I did not comprehend I did.

Foremost, you should know that I know all. I know of Darcy's proposal to you, and your rejection. I know the content of the letter he gave you the following day, in full, for I read it without his knowledge or consent before he sealed it. Knowing this, you will then understand what it took him much time to learn, my most deplorable deed.

I lay in wait for him after he left your side. I've known him since childhood, and I manipulated both the conversation and his emotions until I succeeded in procuring a proposal of marriage from him. Worse, I was fully aware that he regretted it almost immediately, though he staunchly stood by his word. I knew he was still well and truly in love with you.

It is my feeling at the time of writing this, while you are even now in Pemberley as my loyal companion, that he is still fully in love with you and will always be. Me, he was resigned to, then repulsed by, and has now come to tolerate. You, he loves with the entirely of his heart. I could see it the moment his eyes fell upon you in the drive. I knew his love for you when I trapped him into marriage. What I did not realize, until I saw you that day, is that you love him, too.

You may ask, then, why I was so kind to you, why I insisted you stay for dinner. At the time, I told myself it was because I was grateful to you. If you hadn't refused Darcy so unequivocally, he never would have been in such a depressed state and I would not have been able to wring a proposal from him.

As I am most assuredly gone now, and will have brought my sins before the creator, I feel free to admit my second reason. *I enjoyed watching him want you. You, who are so beautiful, so strong and healthy and competent and kind. You are everything I am not, yet I had Darcy and you didn't, and I knew that, no matter how I taunted him with your presence, he would never stray.*

Later, I felt remorse, and desired to make amends. I thought that, if I paid you attention, I could help you win a better husband. Someone to take his place in your heart. I waited until he was away, however, even urging him to stay in London, because I grew fearful the temptation of you would be too great. Please know, though, for my part, I really did feel kindly toward you and have come to cherish your friendship.

All of this, I felt you should know. Consider yourself my confessor, for the unkind harm I have wrought the two of you. I knew you were meant for each other. It is my hope you may still have a long and happy life together. I was but a moment, an important one for me, but one you and Darcy should move past to reach your future.

Sincerely, with love and without regret,
Anne Darcy

Elizabeth stared at the note. Her hands were shaking. Her whole body was shaking. Thoughts tumbled through her head. Anne always knew. He proposed to Anne that very morning. Anne thought Elizabeth was in love with Darcy and that he was in love with her.

She surged to her feet, clutching the pages. There was one thing she was sure Anne was right about, and she could no longer deny it. She could no longer shelter her heart and mind from the truth, holding back out of fear he didn't reciprocate her feelings. No matter how rude he could be, how abrasive or how distant, Elizabeth knew that Anne was right. She was in love with Darcy.

All that remained was to learn if he was in love with her, too. It hardly seemed possible, given his behavior, but she was the one who judged him in love with Anne, seemingly a mistake. Perhaps the inscrutable, maddening, idiot of a man was in love with her, all this time.

Her thoughts were so inflamed, she hardly noticed that she was all but running toward the library. She burst into the room, finding a startled Darcy looking up at her. He sat on a comfortable leather sofa, holding a volume on husbandry. Before he could rise, she stormed forward, thrusting the content of her hand in his face.

"Is this true?" she demanded. Her throat was tight, but she didn't know if it was closing with tears or anger. "Is all of this true?"

He took the papers from her. Maddeningly, he read the letter carefully. He had to keep smoothing the pages, for she'd crumpled them in clenched fists.

Elizabeth stood before him, watching him read. She wanted to reach out and shake him, demanding to know if he loved her. If he did, why was he so distant with her? Why not tell her? Why not exercise the rights of a man over his wife? What sort of cold, calculating, iron souled man was he, that he could walk away from their wedding night when he was in love with her, and not go to her bed when he returned?

He couldn't. No one could. Anne must be mistaken. Elizabeth shouldn't have brought the letter to Darcy. What was she thinking? This would linger between them, mortifying to them both, and only make life worse.

She was about to snatch the letter from him and toss it in the low burning fire when he set it aside. Trembling, Elizabeth watched him stand. He gave her one of his inscrutable looks and crossed to the library door, which she left flung open.

He was leaving. Just leaving. She thought she might faint, or scream, or both.

He shut the door, carefully locking it, and returned to stand before her. She stared up at him in confusion.

"You found this letter?" he asked.

Elizabeth nodded, aware that he was standing much closer than usual. She thought she was used to how tall he was, but so close, he loomed over her. She had to tilt her head back to look at him. "In Anne's desk, in the secret compartment," she said, but her voice came out in a whisper.

"And, obviously, you read it."

She nodded, not trusting sound to emerge should she try to speak. Tilting her head back to look up at him was making her dizzy.

"I can think of only one suitable response to the situation we find ourselves in. Something I think will answer all of your questions, and mine."

The look he gave her was no longer aloof. It wasn't distant, or cold. It smoldered like the coals behind her. Before she could fully gather his intension, his arms were around her, his lips moving against hers. As his mouth caressed hers, he slid one hand into her

78

hair, expertly tugging it loose so he could bury his hand in it. Elizabeth felt her knees buckle at the heat that surged through her, scalded her, but he pressed her so tightly against his body that she couldn't fall. She trembled at his touch, and it was the most wonderful sensation she'd ever felt.

Late that evening, many questioned answered but few words spoken, Elizabeth woke to the marvelous feeling of laying against Darcy's bare chest. They were on the sofa, Elizabeth wrapped in her husband's embrace. Peering up at him, she found him gazing down at her. His deep eyes were so filled with love, she wondered how she could ever have found them expressionless.

"We've both been fools," she said.

Darcy laughed. It was a sound full of joy. "My Elizabeth, how vast my ego should grow if not for you."

"It's true," she said, snuggling closer, letting him ponder her meaning for a moment before elaborating. "I did love you, all this time, which makes me a fool." She looked up at him, begging the question, for the words had not yet passed his lips, though his actions spoke for him.

"And I you, making me an even greater fool," he said.

She frowned, but before she could point out his lack, he put a finger to her lips.

"If you keep after me, I'll get it right one of these days," he said. "What I meant was, I love you, Elizabeth. Then, now and always."

Content, she smiled, snuggling against his strong chest, held secure in his arms.

Epilogue

Darcy felt Elizabeth snuggle next to him. "Happy Birthday," she said sleepily. He took her in his arms and kissed her. The hint of dawn coming through the curtains suggested it was indeed his birthday. It was too early to get up, but there were other things they could do.

Later, Darcy rode around Pemberley for a last look before they went to London. The London and Greenwich Railway was scheduled to start operations. Darcy invested in it and was excited about seeing the first passengers. They would stop at Cambridge to visit their two sons before going on to see their daughter Beth and her husband in London. Georgiana also lived in London and was expecting them to visit. Her second husband was in trade, which shocked Darcy's noble relatives, but Darcy was pleased Georgiana recovered from her bereavement and found someone to love. Darcy and Elizabeth might even visit Rosings, where Kate was complaining that her son kept climbing out of his crib. Darcy thought this was excellent grandparents' revenge, since Kate did the same thing when she was a year old.

Pemberley was oddly empty now that their four children were gone. This trip to London was more about visiting family than overseeing his investment.

More than a week later, after seeing the train belching smoke and passengers, Elizabeth asked Darcy, "Do you think we will be traveling to London by railway in a few years?"

"We probably won't live that long," Darcy said. But he'd already lived longer than Anne predicted. He was fifty-one and his children were essentially grown. He did not have a happy marriage with his first wife, but the second Mrs. Darcy gave him all the happiness he ever hoped for.

The End

Mrs. Bennet's Triumph
A bonus short story

Mrs. Bennet knew life was unfair to her. No one considered her poor nerves. Most of it was Elizabeth's fault. If only she'd married Mr. Collins, Mrs. Bennet wouldn't have to be sharing a bed with Mary. It was most unjust. All five girls could sleep in the two beds in the larger spare room. She was willing to give up the largest bed. But no, everyone was against her. Even Jane said that three in one bed was unreasonable. Elizabeth, Kitty, and Mary were all very thin. Elizabeth should sleep in the center, since she refused Mr. Collins' bed. Surely, the three of them wouldn't mind letting their mother have a bed to herself.

To make matters worse, when this total disregard for her nerves required she take just a little more time for sleep, she found she missed breakfast. Someone should have brought her breakfast. She was still recovering from the terrible carriage accident that killed Mr. Bennet and Lady Lucas. It occurred in May, shortly after Jane returned from London and Elizabeth returned from Kent. Now it was early August. Three months was not enough time to recover. Sir William was barely out of bed, no one hurrying his convalescence or period of mourning, but that viper Charlotte Collins threw her and her girls out of their home.

She would not miss breakfast again. When she arrived, everyone was crowded around the table, but there was still food left. Mr. Phillips said, "Excuse me," stood up and left. How impolite. She'd only just sat down.

"I have to go help Uncle Phillips," Elizabeth said. She left, too. She had no shame. She didn't realize the whole thing was her fault. And what was Mr. Phillips doing to her, anyway? He was making her a clerk. She was copying legal documents and letters for him. Mr. Morris should be doing it. He was Mr. Phillips' clerk. But no, Mr. Morris had more important things to do, according to Mr. Phillips. Elizabeth came back yesterday with ink stains on her hands. How could she find a husband with ink stains?

Jane brought her mending to the table and stayed with Mrs. Bennet until the meal was finished. Jane sewed beautifully, and sewing was acceptable. But she was mending Mr. Phillips' undergarments, and that should be done by a servant. Lydia and Kitty were doing laundry. Who knew if they would get the clothes clean without damaging them? And what would it do to their hands?

Mary was helping in the kitchen. Well, Mary was plain enough so it was unlikely she would find a husband, so it was probably best she make herself useful.

The morning passed slowly. There was nothing to do, no meals to plan, no servants to organize. She couldn't even visit without having the humiliation of going in someone else's carriage, because Mr. Phillips decreed that a carriage was too expensive. She was sure he was making money off their staying. He wouldn't let them stay unless he handled the money. Then, he gave everyone a paltry allowance.

She'd wanted to stay with her brother in London, but it was decided they would stay in Meryton. Her brother had a larger house with more room. All four of her brother's children could stay in one room, giving the Bennets plenty of space. But her brother was so unreasonable. He said he would add to their income, but London was more expensive than Meryton. She complained to her sister, Mrs. Phillips, but even she didn't sympathize with Mrs. Bennet anymore. No one did, and her nerves, her poor nerves, could hardly bear it.

Finally, with the day half done, people behaved in a more civilized manner. Well, Jane was still mending, but at least it wasn't undergarments. Lydia and Kitty finished the laundry and Mary changed out of her flour-covered gown into something nicer. They had callers, Mr. and Mrs. Collins. How dare they call! She couldn't stand the sight of them.

"Good afternoon, Mr. Collins. Are you enjoying Longbourn?" Mrs. Bennet asked, hardly caring if her tone was civil.

Elizabeth slipped in, with ink stained hands, and greeted the guests, as if she had been there all along.

"Yes, Mrs. Bennet. Now that we are in full possession, my wife has agreed with me that I should resign my living in Kent. My noble patroness was unhappy, but I finally persuaded my wife that we do not need her anymore, but that is not what I have come to discuss." He looked around the room at them, like a lord about to confer a favor. It set her teeth on edge. "When I visited you at Longbourn, my intention was to help you by marrying one of your daughters. By a heavenly act, I found my beloved wife. We seemed to be designed for each other. I cannot regret that I didn't marry one of your daughters, but I can take one of them off your hands."

There, Mrs. Bennet thought. He's made his decree. He probably wanted to take her darling Lydia away, but she wouldn't let her sweet girl go to that vipers' den.

"Mrs. Collins said that she would love to have Miss Elizabeth come live with us" Mr. Collins continued, shocking Mrs. Bennet. "We can give her a small allowance, so she will not be a burden on you in any way. It is entirely appropriate, since she is my cousin and my wife's friend. After her stay with us in Hunsford, I know she will fit nicely into our household."

They would give Elizabeth an allowance? Mrs. Bennet was even more stunned, but she'd already made up her mind, before he finished speaking. She wanted nothing from that man and his wife. She opened her mouth to protest. "I don't think…"

Of all the daughters they could choose from, they picked Elizabeth? She was not half as pretty as Jane or as good natured as Lydia. But that was their choice, and they offered an allowance. Mrs. Bennet calculated that her personal allowance would be increased if Elizabeth left. Better yet, Mary would sleep with Jane and she would get a bed to herself. She paused. She realized people were looking at her for her to finish her sentence.

She cleared her throat. "I mean, I think that is very generous of you." There. It even made sense. No one could know she resented Elizabeth. She was glad to get rid of that ungrateful girl. She looked over at Elizabeth, who was always of such a contrary nature, she was sure to find fault with the offer.

"Thank you," Elizabeth said. "I agree with my mother. That is very generous. I am humbly honored at your request and accept with pleasure. I enjoy Charlotte's company."

Mrs. Bennet let go of her fear that Elizabeth would refuse. Finally, the girl showed some sense.

"Miss Elizabeth," Mr. Collins said, peering down his nose at her, "perhaps now you have seen me in marriage, you recognize that your friend has been more fortunate than you— but on this point it will be as well to be silent."

Mrs. Bennet agreed with that, worried his provocations would change Elizabeth's mind, dashing her hopes of a bed to herself and a larger allowance.

"Mr. Collins, I am delighted that my loss was both your and Charlotte's gain. Please believe me when I say that my actions, which you are too generous to resent, made three people happy."

Mary took over copying documents. That girl would never marry, so it didn't really matter. Lydia and Kitty stopped doing laundry and spent their time wandering the streets of Meryton and visiting people within walking distance. Mary and Jane worked harder than ever. Jane did the laundry and the mending and Mary divided her time between the kitchen and Mr. Phillips office. When Mrs. Bennet complained, they pointed out that the agreement was that their allowances would be decreased if the Phillips had to hire more servants, which, of course, was monstrously unfair of Mr. Phillips.

When next Mr. Phillips distributed their weekly allowances, he took it upon himself to give Lydia and Kitty only half the usual amount. "I'm putting the rest aside for the whole family," he said. "It will increase your income a bit. I cannot, in fairness, distribute the same amount of money to you two as I do to your two older sisters, who have worked very hard to see we don't need more servants."

Kitty and Lydia protested, but he was adamant. When they turned beseeching eyes on her, Mrs. Bennet considered protesting on their behalf, but it occurred to her that no one was asking her to do any work, yet she got her full allowance, as was her right. She knew that reprieve was because she grieved for Mr. Bennet and because of her injuries, but those were nearly healed. For the first time in her life, she didn't want to call attention to herself, not wanting anyone else to realize the double standard. Mr. Philips didn't appear to notice her, which, for once, she was grateful for.

About a month after Elizabeth left to live at Longbourn, Sir William Lucas called. He was walking with a cane. Mrs. Bennet wanted to blame him, but seeing his gaunt face, etched with deep lines of pain, she couldn't. She lost her husband, and he lost his wife. "Mrs. Bennet, I've been too unwell to pay my condolences. I'm so sorry about your losing your husband, and if you feel half as sad as I do, you are indeed miserable."

"Thank you, Sir William. If only the carriage wheel hadn't come off where it did," she said, feeling the need to hold back tears. She'd grown accustomed to ignoring the loss of Mr. Bennet, but could not do so when people spoke of it.

"I blame myself and I blame my coachman. It was his job to see the carriage was maintained, but mine to employ a worthy man."

Some of what Jane said about the accident came back to Mrs. Bennet's mind. "But he paid for it with his life. There's no purpose in assigning blame."

"That is generous of you."

His tone warmed so when he said it, his eyes glinting with gratitude, that Mrs. Bennet felt a surge of satisfaction. Was this why Jane was so pleasant to everyone? To secure such regard? Well, Mrs. Bennet thought to herself, I can pretend to be as nice as she is. "There is no point in bitterness," Mrs. Bennet said. "I don't want to live the rest of my life angry."

She didn't mean it before she said it, but when she said it, it made sense. A plan popped into her head. She knew she didn't have the beauty she once had, but she was still a good looking woman. They were both in mourning, which meant nothing could be done for some time, but the groundwork could be laid.

She spent his visit being pleasant to Sir William and even asked him a question which allowed him to repeat the story of his presentation at St. James. Though she'd heard it many times before, she found the familiar story soothing. In spite of her changed circumstances, it was nice to know there were some constants.

Another, less pleasant, constant was Elizabeth's continued disappointment as a daughter. She visited once a week, but they didn't see much of her. Mrs. Bennet didn't mind not having to speak to Elizabeth, but she felt the girl should make more of an effort toward her family. The Collins gave Elizabeth Mary's old room. Mrs. Bennet was torn between the insult of giving her daughter the smallest room and pleasure that Elizabeth didn't benefit too much from her friendship with the wife of the man she should have been smart enough to marry.

Another source of pleasure was an accidental discovery Mrs. Bennet made one morning. If she sat on the floor in the corner of her room, she could hear what transpired in the front parlor. She found this out when she leaned over to pick up her comb, after dropping it. Now, she closed her door and sat there when there were visitors. Once, she overheard Elizabeth and Jane talking. She was pleased that Elizabeth wasn't too happy at Longbourn. She enjoyed Charlotte's company, but found Mr. Collins difficult to bear. Mrs. Bennet didn't like that Elizabeth enjoyed Charlotte's company. Charlotte expelled them from Longbourn. She was glad Elizabeth was having difficulty with Mr. Collins, though. She should suffer, because she was responsible for their situation.

About five months after Mr. Bennet's death, Mrs. Bennet finally overheard something interesting. It was Mary talking, but who was she talking to?

"Don't worry, she's desperate to marry us off."

"But she wants you to marry a gentleman," said a male voice.

"It doesn't matter. Really. I love you and Mama will come around."

"I can't offer you much," he said.

"You'll take over my uncle's practice soon. You're already doing half the work."

A clerk? Mary wanted to marry a clerk. What was his name? Mr. Morris. Mrs. Bennet had met him a few times but was unimpressed. He was an average fellow, not bad looking, no family worth mentioning. He had no money. But if one more daughter could be settled, that was one less worry. A plan came into her head. She might turn this marriage to her family's advantage, after all.

She stood up, careful to do it silently. She spent a couple of minutes seeing to her appearance. It was so hard to do without a maid and with only a small mirror. She casually went downstairs into the parlor. "Hello, Mr. Morris, how nice to see you."

They would agree to what she wanted since she would agree to the marriage.

> *Dear Mr. Bingley,*
> *I hope this letter finds you well. My daughter, Miss Mary Bennet, is marrying Mr. Phillips' clerk, Mr. Henry Morris, on November 26. When the happy couple set the date, I realized it was one year since we last saw you at the delightful ball you had at Netherfield. Since we enjoyed ourselves so much then, I thought I would invite you and your sisters to attend the wedding. Of course, Mr. Hurst and Mr. Darcy are both welcome to attend as well. Please extend this invitation to them, since I don't have their addresses.*

She may as well invite everyone. She didn't care if Mr. Darcy and Mr. Hurst came and she didn't like Mr. Bingley's sisters, but she didn't want it to seem she was trying to bring Mr. Bingley here for Jane.

> *The wedding breakfast will be held at the Phillips house, since Mr. Bennet's untimely death last May forced us to move out of Longbourn.*
> *We are all as well as can be expected, considering*

our reduced circumstances. My eldest daughter, Miss Bennet, is pining more than the rest of us, but she seemed unhappy before Mr. Bennet's death. I hope time will allow her to recover.

She finished the letter properly and signed it. She sent it to Netherfield. It was a gamble, of course, since she didn't know if it would be forwarded. She smiled at the puzzlement of Mary and Mr. Morris about her insistence on that date.

When Sir William called, as he did once a week, she explained the scheme to him. He laughed at her and said, "You will never change."

She knew she had changed. She was poor now and spent a little time humbly helping her sister, even though her arm and shoulder still ached. But she could use that arm. Sir William still needed his cane to walk. Lydia and Kitty were changing, too. After weeks without money, they grudgingly started working around the house, restoring part of their allowances.

As the days passed, she worried about whether the letter was forwarded or not. A week passed, and there was no reply. A second week. Nothing. At least he would write and refuse. As long as he didn't, she had hope.

Before the third week was over, a carriage pulled up. It wasn't Mr. Bingley's carriage. Mr. Darcy got out. What was Mr. Darcy doing here? She'd invited him, but who needed his dour presence? Well, he was a friend of Mr. Bingley, so she should be nice to him. Mr. Bingley got out, too, brightening her spirits considerably. She hastily withdrew from the window and ran to the stairs. "Jane," she called, "come down here at once."

Looking puzzled, Jane came down. Mrs. Bennet wished she had time to make her daughter look more presentable, but there was nothing for it now. Mr. Bingley and Mr. Darcy were already at the door. Mrs. Bennet's sister greeted them, looking quite surprised, and they entered. Mrs. Bennet allowed her sister the privilege, as hostess. She found she no longer resented it. She was grateful they took her in. It was bitter that she was a poor relative, but embracing her bitterness only made her unhappy, so she was learning to let it go.

She followed Mr. Bingley's gaze to Jane. Her hands were red from doing laundry and her clothing was wearing out, in spite of careful mending. Jane and Mary retained their full allowances, but Mrs. Bennet had to give Lydia and Kitty some of hers, since the poor girls had nothing to wear. As it was, they each could only buy one new dress of half-mourning. What a waste, to buy a grey dress, but unrelieved black was so depressing.

The meeting went as well as could be expected. Both men were polite and stayed a half an hour. Mr. Darcy asked after Elizabeth, which surprised Mrs. Bennet. He usually wasn't that polite. When the correct half hour was over, Mr. Darcy, of all people, suggested they should drive Jane over to Longbourn so she could visit Elizabeth, because he knew how close the two of them were. Surprised at his unusual curtesy, she encouraged the trip.

The next several days were confusing to Mrs. Bennet. She learned that Mr. Darcy visited the Collins several times. She had no idea what they had in common. Mr. Bingley came and visited, which made much more sense. Everyone conspired to allow him time alone with Jane. Mrs. Bennet listened from her post in her room and heard him commiserate with Jane on her reddened hands. Being Jane, she made light of it. Why couldn't she complain so he could rescue her?

Mary's wedding was fast approaching and still none of her schemes had come to fruition. She complained to Sir William on one of his many visits. "When the wedding is over, Mr. Bingley will probably go back to London. Why can't he propose now?"

"He may think it's too soon after her father's death," Sir William replied.

"Mr. Bennet and Lady Lucas died seven months ago. Jane isn't growing younger and her hands and clothing will only get worse. He must propose soon, before she loses her grace. We all have to go on living, after all."

"Yes, we do."

Mary was married, the wedding breakfast eaten and the happy couple gone to his lodgings. Mrs. Bennet wondered if Mr. Bingley would go back to London. Was her letter all for nothing? Sir William came over and she indulged herself in a discourse about how vexing it was that Mr. Bingley wasn't behaving as she'd hoped when she sent the letter. After she finished, she said, "I tried to do what was best for Jane. I may not have succeeded, but I had to try. With all her beauty, I hate to see her marry someone like Mary's husband. I know he's a good man and Mr. Phillips told me he will be a good lawyer, but I wanted better for Jane."

"Of course you did. We all want better for our children."

"And for ourselves," she said. "I've been selfish. I wanted

comfort. Thank you for listening. You're too kind to me, Sir William." She looked away, acting as if she were musing, but saying words she'd carefully planned. "I now know my relatives won't let me starve, but I'll never be mistress of Longbourn again. I miss it. But I have to live with what I've got. Lydia and Kitty are learning that, too. Mr. Phillips gave them their full allowances last week." She looked at her old friend. "Here I am complaining, and you've lost your wife and you walk with limp. You have as much to complain about as I do." Make it work, she thought. It has to work.

A scant half hour later, Mr. Darcy and Mr. Bingley came for a visit. Elizabeth and Jane were with them. From the look on Jane's face, Mrs. Bennet could tell that Mr. Bingley proposed. Oddly enough, Elizabeth had a similar look of happiness. Mrs. Bennet could tell that Jane wanted to wait until Sir William left, but she couldn't. She burst out her good news. After the warm congratulations, Elizabeth announced she had accepted a proposal from Mr. Darcy. Mrs. Bennet was stunned. She'd had no inkling he was interested in Elizabeth.

It took her a couple of minutes to understand, but when she did, she gave her consent and congratulations. "My dearest, sweetest Elizabeth! What wonderful news. How clever of you."

She wanted to go on in that vein, but Elizabeth stood up and came over to kiss her cheek. Mrs. Bennet hoped Elizabeth knew she should be grateful. If Mrs. Bennet hadn't planned the whole thing by inviting Mr. Darcy to the wedding, this would never have happened.

She gazed up at Elizabeth, noticing how very pretty she was today. In fact, Elizabeth was, in many ways, prettier even than Jane or Lydia. When she was being clever about important things, Elizabeth was Mrs. Bennet's favorite daughter. She was pleased she worked so hard to see Elizabeth was happy.

Sir William suggested they get out the wine and toast the happy couples. When they toasted Jane and Mr. Bingley, and then Elizabeth and Mr. Darcy, Sir William said, looking at Mrs. Bennet, "And now, I would like to toast the next Lady Lucas."

Mrs. Bennet smiled. When they married in five months, she would have something her daughters never would have: a title.

The End

Made in the USA
Lexington, KY
23 August 2014